THE PERFECT COVER

CHARLOTTE BYRD

CHARLOTTE BYRD
dangerously addictive

Copyright © 2020 by Charlotte Byrd, LLC.

All rights reserved.

Proofreaders:

Julie Deaton, Deaton Author Services, https://www.facebook.com/jdproofs/

Renee Waring, Guardian Proofreading Services, https://www.facebook.com/GuardianProofreadingServices

Savanah Cotton, Cotton's Incision Editing, https://www.facebook.com/Cottons-Incision-Editing-512917856115256/

Cover Design: Charlotte Byrd

No part of this book may be reproduced in any form or by any electronic or mechanical means, including information storage and retrieval systems, without written permission from the author, except for the use of brief quotations in a book review.

This book is a word of fiction. Names, characters, places, and incidents are either products of the author's imagination or are used fictitiously. Any resemblance to actual persons, living or dead, events, or locales is entirely coincidental. The author acknowledges the trademarked status and trademark owners of various products referenced in this work of fiction, which have been used without permission. The publication/use of these trademarks is not authorized, associated with, or sponsored by the trademark owners.

Visit my website at www.charlotte-byrd.com

Created with Vellum

PRAISE FOR CHARLOTTE BYRD

"BEST AUTHOR YET! Charlotte has done it again! There is a reason she is an amazing author and she continues to prove it! I was definitely not disappointed in this series!!"
★★★★★

"LOVE!!! I loved this book and the whole series!!! I just wish it didn't have to end. I am definitely a fan for life!!! ★★★★★

"Extremely captivating, sexy, steamy, intriguing, and intense!" ★★★★★

"Addictive and impossible to put down."
★★★★★

"What a magnificent story from the 1st book through book 6 it never slowed down always surprising the reader in one way or the other. Nicholas and Olive's paths crossed in a most unorthodox way and that's how their story begins it's exhilarating with that nail biting suspense that keeps you riding on the edge the whole series. You'll love it!" ★★★★★

"What is Love Worth. This is a great epic ending to this series. Nicholas and Olive have a deep connection and the mystery surrounding the deaths of the people he is accused of murdering is to be read. Olive is one strong woman with deep convictions. The twists, angst, confusion is all put together to make this worthwhile read." ★★★★★

"Fast-paced romantic suspense filled with twists and turns, danger, betrayal, and so much more." ★★★★★

"Decadent, delicious, & dangerously addictive!" - Amazon Review ★★★★★

"Titillation so masterfully woven, no reader can resist its pull. A MUST-BUY!" - Bobbi Koe, Amazon Review ★★★★★

"Captivating!" - Crystal Jones, Amazon Review ★★★★★

"Sexy, secretive, pulsating chemistry…" - Mrs. K, Amazon Reviewer ★★★★★

"Charlotte Byrd is a brilliant writer. I've read loads and I've laughed and cried. She writes a balanced book with brilliant characters. Well done!" -Amazon Review ★★★★★

"Hot, steamy, and a great storyline." - Christine Reese ★★★★★

"My oh my....Charlotte has made me a fan for life." - JJ, Amazon Reviewer ★★★★★

"Wow. Just wow. Charlotte Byrd leaves me speechless and humble… It definitely kept me on the edge of my seat. Once you pick it up, you won't put it down." - Amazon Review ★★★★★

" Intrigue, lust, and great characters...what more could you ask for?!" - Dragonfly Lady ★★★★★

WANT TO BE THE FIRST TO KNOW ABOUT MY UPCOMING SALES, NEW RELEASES AND EXCLUSIVE GIVEAWAYS?

Sign up for my newsletter: https://www.subscribepage.com/byrdVIPList

Join my Facebook Group: https://www.facebook.com/groups/276340079439433/

Bonus Points: Follow me on BookBub and Goodreads!

ABOUT CHARLOTTE BYRD

Charlotte Byrd is the bestselling author of romantic suspense novels. She has sold over 700,000 books and has been translated into five languages.

She lives near Palm Springs, California with her husband, son, and a toy Australian Shepherd who hates water. Charlotte is addicted to books and Netflix and she loves hot weather and crystal blue water.

Write her here:
charlotte@charlotte-byrd.com
Check out her books here:
www.charlotte-byrd.com
Connect with her here:
www.facebook.com/charlottebyrdbooks
www.instagram.com/charlottebyrdbooks
www.twitter.com/byrdauthor

Sign up for my newsletter: https://www.subscribepage.com/byrdVIPList

Join my Facebook Group: https://www.facebook.com/groups/276340079439433/

Bonus Points: Follow me on BookBub and Goodreads!

facebook.com/charlottebyrdbooks
twitter.com/byrdauthor
instagram.com/charlottebyrdbooks
bookbub.com/profile/charlotte-byrd

ALSO BY CHARLOTTE BYRD

All books are available at ALL major retailers! If you can't find it, please email me at charlotte@charlotte-byrd.com

The Perfect Stranger Series
The Perfect Stranger
The Perfect Cover
The Perfect Lie
The Perfect Life
The Perfect Getaway
The Perfect Couple

All the Lies Series
All the Lies

All the Secrets
All the Doubts
All the Truths
All the Promises
All the Hopes

Tell me Series
Tell Me to Stop
Tell Me to Go
Tell Me to Stay
Tell Me to Run
Tell Me to Fight
Tell Me to Lie

Wedlocked Trilogy
Dangerous Engagement
Lethal Wedding
Fatal Wedding

Tangled Series
Tangled up in Ice
Tangled up in Pain
Tangled up in Lace
Tangled up in Hate
Tangled up in Love

The Perfect Cover

Black Series
Black Edge
Black Rules
Black Bounds
Black Contract
Black Limit

Not into you Duet
Not into you
Still not into you

Lavish Trilogy
Lavish Lies
Lavish Betrayal
Lavish Obsession

Standalone Novels
Dressing Mr. Dalton
Debt
Offer
Unknown

THE PERFECT COVER

When Tyler McDermott escapes from prison, he takes me hostage. No, I do not fall in love with my captor.

Tyler is an innocent man who was framed for a heinous double murder.

Of course, I do not know that yet.

All that I know is that he has a knife to my throat. All that I know is that if I want to live, I have to let him in.

This simple act of courage will change my safe life forever and show me that true love is possible after all.

But what happens when that love is not enough?

1

TYLER

WHEN I LEAVE...

Last night was my thank you to Isabelle for everything she had done for me.

Last night was also my goodbye.

I knew I was going to leave as soon as we got to Ohio, the first place we stopped. I needed her help to get out of her neighborhood and all of the roads that were blocked. I needed to get at least a state away.

But after that?

I can't have her endangering her life for me anymore.

I know that Isabelle won't let me leave on my own. I know that she wants to protect me, but I can't let her.

This is one of the most difficult things I've ever had to endure and that includes identifying my wife's dead body, standing in the courtroom, and being convicted of a murder that I didn't commit.

Isabelle and I leave in the middle of the night. Blackness is still hanging in the air all around us.

I give her a kiss right before I get into the trunk of the 2002 Honda Accord that she bought from an ad on Craigslist. No one knows that this is the car that she's driving and it's going to be a while before all of the official forms are filed with the state in her name.

Standing in her garage, I press my lips softly to hers. She's shivering. I rub her shoulders to warm her up, but the goose bumps don't go away.

She's not cold. She's nervous.

"It's going to be okay," I whisper.

She gives me a slight nod and then gets up on her tiptoes to kiss me again. After a moment, we just hold each other in our arms.

It's hard to explain how surprised I am that any of this is happening. When I first escaped from a maximum-security prison and hid in the home of the woman I only knew as a child, I had hoped that I could keep her sequestered in her room so that she wouldn't find out my identity.

When that didn't work and she recognized me, I had no choice but to tell her the truth.

I thought that she wouldn't believe me. I had been convicted of killing my wife, her boyfriend, and her unborn child, the child that I had no knowledge of. The only thing I knew was that my wife's lover was my partner and he had just taken the business from me. Unfortunately, the prosecutor used that as motive. Therefore, I must have done it.

The cops agreed and didn't investigate. My wife's murderer is still at-large and I was sentenced to life in prison.

No one believed me when I tried to tell them I was innocent.

No one except for Isabelle.

Isabelle knew me when I was barely a teenager. We were best friends and we had feelings for each other but neither of us admitted it out loud. She knew who I was at my core and she knew that I did not commit those crimes. I don't know why she believed me, but she did and for that I will be eternally grateful.

However, her faith in me doesn't change my circumstances. Every law enforcement officer in the Tri-state area is looking for me and I had gotten injured trying to escape. I thought that hiding out at her home would relieve some of the pressure, but I quickly realized that they were circling in on me.

There are police officers patrolling all the streets in her neighborhood and even pulling people and cars over to give out WANTED flyers with our pictures. There is a $100,000 reward available to anyone who can give the authorities any information leading to our arrests.

There's an actual bounty on my head.

When I was studying at the University of Pennsylvania and starting my hedge fund, making millions of dollars in the process, I never suspected that I would ever be in this situation; hiding out in the trunk of a car and crossing state lines with the only person who believes in my innocence.

So, why am I leaving her?

I have thought about this a hundred

different times and imagined a hundred different scenarios. I need to protect Isabelle, but I also need to get out.

She bought a car that she registered in her name and she took out cash from the bank, all of the savings that she has in the world. I came to her without a penny to my name and I'm leaving with new clothes, a car, a burner phone, and five thousand dollars. And I didn't need to steal any of it.

The only reason I'm taking it, borrowing it, whatever you want to call it, is that I need to protect her. I need her to go back home and to live her life just like she did before.

It's cold back here.

The air is still and stale.

It's dark.

We drive for a long time without stopping and I know that no one suspects a thing. The longer we drive, the more I wonder whether I'm even doing the right thing.

It's not that I don't want to be with her. In fact, I want to be with her more than I ever wanted anything. Probably more than I even want freedom, and that's what makes it so scary.

The cops who found Lester, one of my partners, the guy whose cell was right next to mine, shot him. They executed him without even trying to arrest him. They didn't report that on the news, but I know that's what happened. That's usually what happens with everyone who is deemed armed and dangerous.

Since I love Isabelle, I can't let that happen to her. I can't put her life in danger like that.

The car comes to a stop and she hits the steering wheel three times with a loud bang that I hear all the way in the back.

This is my signal.

I know that everything is fine and that she's just pulling over to let me out.

I feel the outside of my pocket and the jeans that she got me at T.J. Maxx. I trace the outline of the folded up letter that I had written her.

Here, I tried to explain and apologize for everything. I also left her a thousand dollars so that she can get an Uber to a car rental place and then rent a car to get back home.

In the letter, I lay it all out and I tell her not to worry. I promise that I will get in contact as soon as I have everything set out west.

After I emerge from the trunk, in the back of a gas station somewhere along the interstate, I quickly get into the passenger seat so that no one spots me. Wearing a hat that I pull over my eyebrows and popping up the collar to my jacket, I hope that there are no cameras back here and, if there are any, that they don't see me.

Isabelle says that she's going to get something from the store and asks what I want. I tell her to surprise me and she waves goodbye.

When I give her a hug, I slip the letter into her purse and make sure that she takes it, even when she just wants to take her wallet.

She doesn't think anything of it at the moment, but I know that she will as soon as she comes out.

When she disappears around the corner of the convenience store, I start the car and pull away.

2

ISABELLE

WHEN I SEE HIM...

The door closes behind me, making a loud dinging sound before it shuts. The chill of the early morning slams into my lungs as I take a breath and look for Tyler.

I go back to where I left the car. It's not there.

Uncertain as to what to do, I stand holding everything that I had bought in my arms and listen to the uncomfortable crinkling sound of the plastic bag of potato chips.

When the wind picks up, I grasp the stuff tighter, wondering if it's the only thing I have.

"Tyler, where are you?" I whisper.

My chest tightens as my pulse accelerates.

Was it a police officer?

Did they take him already?

No.

If it had to do with law enforcement, then this place would be crawling with them. They'd be blaring their lights and pointing their guns in my face.

At least, that's what happens on television and everything that happens on television happens in real life, right?

I laugh.

Maybe it was the federal marshals who snagged him. That's who looks for escaped convicts after all. Maybe they trailed us and took him while I was inside.

But wouldn't they also have questions for me?

Then something else occurs to me.

What if all of this had been a set-up?

What if Tyler just used me to get this car and some money to get the fuck out of here?

Standing in front of the convenience store, my feet suddenly become too heavy to lift. I try to move but I'm either too weak or the gravitational pull of the Earth is too strong. In either case, I'm stuck.

"Miss, are you okay?" someone asks.

I saw him go in a few minutes ago, and now he's on his way out.

"Did something happen to your car?" he asks. "Did someone take your wallet?"

Soundly, I snap out of my daze and feel around for the bag near my waist.

"No, I'm fine," I say quickly, pointing to my cross-body purse.

So, that's why Tyler said that.

A light bulb goes off in my head.

It seemed odd that he handed it to me when I already had my wallet, but I guess he didn't want to leave me here without... anything.

The Good Samaritan walks away from me, relieved that his help is no longer needed.

I shift my weight from one foot to another as I feel my body start to wake up from the shock.

Now, I have to figure out what to do.

I reach over to my purse and unzip it. I'm in another state and it's going to cost some money to get back.

But do I have enough?

Searching through my bag, I see a folded up piece of paper. It's a letter and it's from him.

Tyler left me.

The world tilts on its axis.

And then I see him.

He pulls up to the curb and gives me that beautiful open mouth smile.

Is this really him? Is this Tyler McDermott?

Cracking the passenger window, he says, "Get in."

I feel like the wind has just been knocked out of me.

Questioning everything that just happened, I wonder if I had made a mistake.

"Where did you go?" I ask and shut the door behind me.

Why is he back?

What about everything that he had written?

"What do you mean?" Tyler asks as if nothing had happened, even adding a casual shrug. "I just drove around while you shopped. I didn't want the camera to focus in on our car or me in particular. I thought that we would be harder to track this way."

Of course, yes, that makes sense.

A wave of relief rushes over me. When I give him a slight nod, he grabs a bag of pretzels from my cold hands and pulls out onto the highway.

I DON'T BRING up the letter or that I had seen it. I just turn up Bob Dylan and lose myself in the lyrics.

Did I actually read what I think I did?
Was it real?

I look into my purse and feel around for the letter. In the back pocket, I find its thick outline, where it is bent in half.

We drive for a while and I start to doze off. I've always been the type of person who needs plenty of sleep just to function through the day. Getting up so early and in the middle of the night has worn me out. At first, I fight my tiredness, but then I close my eyes and drift off, admitting defeat.

I don't know how much time passes, but it

feels like none at all when suddenly, I see his hand rummaging through the bag in my lap.

Is this a dream?

When I open my eyes, it all rushes back to me.

"What are you doing?" I ask.

"Nothing," Tyler says a little too quickly, like a man who has been caught doing something illicit. "I was just trying to move that so you would be more comfortable."

I don't believe him.

Of course not.

He's lying but I'm lying, too.

We drive for another hour and then another one. I want to bring up the letter, but I'm too tired from the day to talk about anything that serious. I need more sleep.

Later that night, we pull into a Motel 6. It's a double-decker building with each room's front door going straight outside. There's a Denny's across the street and we talk about getting some food, but I'm not in the mood for anything fast, greasy, or with meat. Luckily, when I check my phone, I learn that there's a Trader Joe's only ten minutes away.

The Perfect Cover

I ask Tyler what he wants and he just gives me a big over-exaggerated shrug.

"Whatever you're going to get is fine," he says with a tone of defeat.

Does he know what I'm thinking of doing? How could he not?

I'm tempted to bring up the letter, but again, I hesitate.

Instead, I wait for him to stop me from going, but he doesn't.

He acts like he trusts me even though he probably shouldn't.

At Trader Joe's, I get a cart full of food. It's cheaper and will last a lot longer than roadside diner food, but it's not just the money that I'm worried about. I come here to get away from him. I come here to try to make up my mind about what to do.

Tyler tried to leave me and then changed his mind.

Now it's my turn to decide if I should go home.

While standing in line, I get a call from work. It's Trisha. Her voice is peppy and sweet as always. I have worked for her for almost a year and while she doesn't know all the details about my anxieties and fears, she knows that I'm not exactly all there. She also knows that I don't take spontaneous road trips.

"Hey there," I say, forcing a smile on my face.

"How are you?"

"Yeah, I'm good," I mumble. "I just needed to get some time off."

I'm not sure if I come off believable, but I hope so.

"Yes, I know. Normally, it's no problem at all, but with Lindsey's due date coming up and with all the uncertainty about her maternity leave, I just wish that you could have chosen a better time for this."

Trisha stops short of calling me an asshole, a name that I rightly deserve. Of course, I already know all of this and I wish this could've happened any time but now.

"I know that this is a really big inconvenience, but I've just had some stuff come up and I needed a break, okay? I'll be back in ten days."

This is the plan so far. My trip should last

a week. In that time, Tyler and I will drive out west and then I'll come back. But now...

"I know but we really need your help-" Trisha starts to say, but I cut her off and promise to call back later.

The checkout clerk scans all of my chips and snacks as well as vegan cheeses and a quart of dairy-free ice cream. We don't have a fridge in the car, but it probably won't last me through the evening.

I drive back to the motel room and open the door using my key card.

"You're back?" Tyler asks, sitting up in the bed, looking astonished.

I nod, wincing under the weight of the groceries.

"I was certain that I would never see you again," he says, helping me with the bags.

"Well, I was certain that I would never see you again at the gas station, so imagine my surprise."

The silly smile vanishes from his face. He stares at me without breaking eye contact.

"Oh, you didn't know about that? You didn't think that I read your letter?"

He darts his eyes away, but only for a moment.

"You tried to take the letter away from me while I was sleeping." I continue my assault.

"What were you doing?" I ask. "It better be the truth. If you tell me one more bullshit lie, then I'm fucking out of here."

3

ISABELLE

WHEN WE TALK...

Tyler closes his eyes and licks his lips. He opens his mouth like he's about to say something, but then inhales a little breath and stops himself. I hope he knows that I'm serious. I hope he knows that if he doesn't tell me the truth, then I won't continue on this journey with him for another mile.

"Is this why you went to the store?" he asks, even though he knows the answer.

"I had to think. I read the letter and I know what it says. You were going to leave me."

"I know, I was, but since you read the

letter you know the truth. Everything in the letter is the truth."

"What was I supposed to do? After you left me at the gas station?"

He licks his lips again and looks down at the floor.

"Did you not finish reading it?"

"Of course I did," I say, nodding vigorously. "You left me $1,000. You told me to take an Uber to the nearest car rental place. On paper, it was all going to work out perfectly, wasn't it?"

"Why wouldn't it work out that way?"

"The world doesn't work like that. It's not just about the logistics of the whole thing, there are other things at play.

"I was alone. Yes, I have money but I need...." I stop short of saying that I needed *him*. "We made all these plans and we were going to start this new life."

"We were never going to start a life together. I can't let that happen, Isabelle. You mean the world to me. I fucking love you. That means that I can't have anything happening to you. The federal marshals are after me. My face is plastered on every television screen in the nation. You would have to live under a rock to not know what I look like or how much money my reward is. You really think that I'm going to get away with this?"

"How many times are you going to question that? I mean, what are we even doing if you don't believe that you're going to get away? Why did you even try to escape? What's the fucking point?"

Anger starts to rise up within me again.

"Listen, I'll try to explain why I left that letter, but there's something else that you need to know."

I cross my arms and turn away from him. I told him that I want to hear the truth and that I would hear him out, but now I am too angry, upset, and pissed off.

"I can't believe you were just going to leave me there. I mean, how am I going to *trust* you again?"

Tyler shakes his head and says, "Maybe you shouldn't."

He takes a step closer to me and puts his arms around mine. "You have to hear me out though."

I shake my head.

He bends his head down and presses his lips to my neck.

They are cool to the touch. Soft and silky.

When I feel his tongue on my skin, shivers run up my spine. I don't want to hear anything that he has to say and yet I can't *not* listen.

"I shouldn't have left. It is one of the million mistakes that I have made in my life so far. I'm sure that I'm going to make more. People act like they can live this life with no regrets, but that's just a farce. It's fucking make-believe.

"It's impossible to live that way. Every day that you make a decision, any number of things can happen. I wrote that letter to protect you. I needed you to drive me out of the city, out of your development where the cops were checking every car. I needed your help, but after that? I was worried about you.

"You shouldn't risk your life to protect me. I'm a scumbag. I didn't kill Sarah or Greg, but that doesn't make me a non-shitty person. It is my cross to bear and I'm trying to gain my own freedom but the only thing that would happen to you is that they would put you in prison for helping me. I don't want to see that happen."

I look up at Tyler and our eyes meet. I can't look away. I know that every word of what he is saying is the truth, the whole truth, and nothing but the truth.

He bends down and puts his lips onto mine. I open my mouth and kiss him back.

Our arms look for each other's and our fingers intertwine. He presses his body to mine and I push back at him. My hands make their way up his neck and bury themselves in his hair. He grabs me by my ponytail and tugs down.

With my head tilted back, he kisses my exposed neck. His mouth generates heat that overwhelms me. I wrap my leg around him, pulling him closer to me. His hands start to move up and down my body, feverishly, almost as if they are in search of something.

My clothes can't come off fast enough.

I raise my arms up as he pulls off my shirt and then I tug at his. When he tries to lean over and kiss the top of my breasts, I push him away for a moment and run my fingers up and down his hard, chiseled body.

"You're so hot," I whisper.

"Not as hot as you are," he says.

Suddenly, I get very self-conscious about my stomach and I suck it in a little bit, but he shakes his head, so I stop.

He runs his fingers up and down my side, then leans over and unclasps my bra. We make our way to the bed where he pushes me down and pulls off my leggings.

Leaning over me, he unbuckles his pants and lets them slide all the way down to the floor. I glance down at his large cock and my mouth waters for it.

When I lean over and rub my hands around it, I glance up and see him close his eyes. When I replace my hands with my mouth, he tilts his head back slowly.

A few moments later, he pulls away and flips me over onto my stomach.

"I want you," he whispers in my ear.

"I want you, too," I whisper back even though my mouth is muffled by the pillow.

My desire for him burns in the center of my core and I get wetter and wetter. I open my legs wide and stick my butt in the air, and he comes from behind and slides in.

As soon as I take him all the way inside, suddenly the world falls away and nothing else exists except for the two of us.

Our movements are slow at first.

Easy-going and relaxed.

Then something starts to build within and I begin to crave him. I move my body back and forth increasing the speed of each thrust. Grabbing onto my hips, he starts to take control. He knows exactly what I want and he's going to give it to me.

A few moments later, the energy between us explodes almost at the same time. A wave of pleasure overwhelms my senses. I curl my toes and let myself go. He collapses on top of me and I breathe hard into the sheets and pillows underneath.

We stay there for some time, reveling in the beauty of what just happened. Some people might think this is a sin, but I see it as an expression of love with a man who completes me.

"Oh my God," I whisper, putting my hand over my mouth.

"What's wrong?" Tyler asks, pulling out.

"We didn't use anything," I gasp.

My voice is barely audible and my chest tightens out of fear.

"What are you talking about?" He laughs. "I slipped on a condom right before. I would never go bareback without your permission."

I let out a sigh of relief and smile.

4

TYLER

AFTER...

I've never had this kind of sexual chemistry with anyone before. With my wife, we had good sex, but we were never drawn to each other this way. I don't know why we got married, except that it seemed like something that everyone was doing.

Isabelle asks me all about it as we lie in each other's arms, holding on to one another in the glow of what we'd just done.

"So, how did it happen?" she asks again. "You loved her, of course, right?"

"Yes, I did," I say, thinking back to that kid that went to Penn who got into a relationship with a girl who lived on his floor and somehow never got out of it.

"I met her at orientation," I say quietly. "She had a really big fun side and she always knew how to laugh. We had the same group of friends. We all hung out together and somehow everyone separated into couples. After graduation, all of our friends started to get married. One engagement followed another. We lived together and I knew that she expected that from me as well. I loved her and I had no reason to *not* get her an engagement ring."

Isabelle gives me a nod as if she understands, but the truth is that I hardly understand it myself.

Why would someone marry someone that they had no interest in being married to?

"Do you think you'll ever get married again?" she asks.

I look down at her.

She narrows her eyes in that cunning analyzing sort of way.

"Is that a proposal?" I ask.

Her eyes turn into big round saucers as a wave of surprise rushes over her.

"No, absolutely not," she says.

"I'm just kidding," I say, smiling with the corner of my lips. "I'd marry you in a second."

I let the line hang there, realizing that it is not even an exaggeration of the truth.

"Tell me something real," she says.

I know that I can't, or shouldn't, repeat myself.

"Sarah and I were very different people. We wanted very different things in the world. It's not that I didn't want a wife and a family. It's that I didn't want it with her. It's a really cruel thing to say, but I used to think that I was just not the marrying type. I just didn't want to be married, but the truth is that I just didn't want to be married to *her*."

"So, why *did* you marry her?"

"I don't know," I say.

She pulls away from me and sits up, covering her breasts with the barely threaded Motel 6 sheet.

"It just seemed like the polite thing to do," I finally say. "I hate how coldhearted and detached I sound, but that's the truth. That's what happened. All of our friends were getting married and I didn't want to *not* propose and make her feel like there was something wrong with our relationship. The truth was that there was nothing wrong with our relationship. I loved her and she loved me and I wanted to be with her. Then after a while, I didn't want to be with her anymore and I didn't know how to stop the marriage."

"When was this?" she asks.

"It was about a year before her murder. Things had been off for a while. We became ships passing in the night. I started spending more time at work. I wanted to get my own apartment but I didn't want to break her heart. I kept postponing telling her. I kept spending more and more time in the office. After a while, I just didn't come home at all."

"You had no idea that she was having an affair?"

I shake my head and say, "Honestly, it would have been a relief to find out. Of course, I didn't want her to sleep with Greg, but it would've made our conversation a lot easier."

We talk about this and a lot more things while lying in bed that evening, without getting dressed. I haven't talked to anyone about this before.

Isabelle is so easy to talk to that the words just keep spilling out of me.

I tell her the truth about anything she asks.

Why bother lying? If I can't tell the truth now, when could I?

After a little while, my stomach starts to growl and I bite into one of the sandwiches that she'd gotten from the store.

Her phone rings and after looking at the screen, she sighs and answers.

"Hi, Trisha," she says in a fake upbeat tone that sounds foreign.

"Yeah, I know that it's difficult, but like I said before, I really need this time off."

Suddenly the screen lights up and makes a little dinging sound. She looks at it and says that she can't FaceTime now, but when she goes to hit ignore, she accidentally hits accept and I have only a moment to duck out of the way.

"Hey, you scared me," Isabelle says, standing up quickly to make sure that the screen is pointed away from me.

She puts her finger up in the air to tell me to stand still and be quiet.

"I just wanted to make sure that you're okay," Trisha says.

She has a concerned, motherly type of voice which is a bit overbearing.

"Yes, I'm fine, just having some dinner."

Isabelle flips the phone around to show her the food piled up on the dining table as proof.

"Okay, good, you just really scared me. I know that you don't go out often and you're not very social. Then suddenly I get this message from you saying that you're going to be away for a while and that you need a break."

"I appreciate you worrying about me," Isabelle says with a chuckle.

"Besides, with everything on the news about the prison escape…I just had to make sure that you are safe."

Isabelle freezes on the spot. My breath gets lodged in my throat as I stand motionless directly in front of her, praying that she doesn't turn the camera around and expose me.

"What do you mean?" Isabelle says with a laugh. "Did you think that one of them came to my house and kidnapped me and this whole thing is just some elaborate lie?"

"Okay," Trisha says with exasperation.

I can almost hear her hands going up in the air, a signal of giving up.

"I know, I'm a fool. I'm the one who always gets freaked out by every new thing on the news, but don't be mad at me for being worried about you. You're a single woman. You live alone. You have certain patterns, and then suddenly you just decide to take off? I wanted to see your face to make sure that everything is fine."

I watch Isabelle try to comfort herself by rubbing one shoulder with her hand while holding the phone in the other.

"I know that I should've been more honest…" she says, sitting down on the edge of the bed. "I just couldn't. I've had a lot of personal problems, as you know, and I didn't want you to… Disapprove."

"Why would I disapprove?"

"I don't know. The truth is that everything is fine. I'm just taking some me time. I know that it's not ideal, but if there is something that I can do to make up for it, let me know."

That's the sort of thing that you say when you really don't expect anyone to take you up on the offer. Trisha, however, has other plans.

"Well, actually, I was wondering if you could still do some of your appointments while you're away? I've talked to a few of your clients like Robert's mom, Mason's mom, and Tommy's mom. They all said that they would have no problem trying out speech therapy using Zoom, FaceTime, or whatever program you would prefer. They just don't want to stop going and get behind."

Isabelle's face clenches up. She's stuck. It's practically impossible to get out of a teleconference and Trisha knows this. Isabelle forces a smile and finally agrees.

"I can't believe that she did that to me," she says after hanging up. Shaking her head, she goes straight to the grocery haul and pulls out a bottle of Pinot Gris.

"Of course, I *can't* say no to online teaching. We can arrange the time around my schedule," she says sarcastically. "I'm so… agh! I'm aggravated."

When I attempt to put my arm around her, she shrugs it off and continues to vent.

5

ISABELLE

WHEN I HANG UP...

I hate the way that Trisha trapped me, but I guess I should've seen it coming. On the positive side, I get to still collect my paycheck while I'm on this little road trip and hopefully the boys won't fall too far behind.

It's difficult to get a substitute for what I do. The kids are two to five years old and they connect with you. If you leave, or if you need to take a week off, they don't understand why.

They're used to you and they want what they're used to. Mason would have been a lot more amenable to a change but the other two? I'm not so sure.

I talk to Tyler about this and he calms me down by telling me that it's going to be okay.

His voice is soft and soothing.

He pushes away all the negative thoughts. It's not that I don't like her. I do, but she can be a little bit overbearing and unaccommodating at times.

It's her business. She runs it with a smile and an iron fist.

Why haven't I looked for work elsewhere? I did, but only briefly. The drive was always too far and I wasn't sure if the other bosses would be any more accommodating than Trisha. Besides, until this trip, I never needed any kind of accommodation.

After eating dinner in bed and watching some late-night TV, Tyler falls asleep and starts to snore. I, on the other hand, can't get my head to stop from spinning.

I know that looking on my phone and reading the news is not going to help, but I'm drawn to it like an addict to the pipe.

I open Google News and search for Tyler's name. One article after another pops up, but none of them say anything particularly illuminating.

I turn to Twitter. I wouldn't say that I have much faith in Twitter, but on occasion, whenever there's any sort of local emergency, I like to get some input from there just in case there are some voices that aren't being amplified by traditional news sources. Unfortunately, most of the posts are retweets of articles from the Pittsburgh Post-Gazette and the Pittsburgh Tribune.

All of the stories say that the suspects are armed and dangerous. Of course, they have no confirmation of that because no one knows where they are, but that doesn't stop the reporters from reporting that.

It's probably what the police told them. Besides, no one's going to take an escapee seriously if they're not armed and dangerous, right?

I should stop reading this stuff, I say to myself, but I can't force myself to close the tab. One article becomes another and another.

I don't know what I'm searching for, but somehow, I end up on a legal blog analyzing the case against Tyler. It belongs to a defense attorney who is arguing against his conviction.

He also has a few YouTube videos up

where he makes his case for why Tyler is innocent. I watch a few of the videos, becoming more and more convinced that the feeling that I have about Tyler is true. The attorney points out all the flaws in the prosecution's case, the gaps, the reasoning, and the evidence, all of the things that Tyler has never mentioned.

I wonder why not?

My phone dings and I look down at the screen. It's another unlisted number. I don't answer and wait for the texts. The first one arrives a few moments later, but much to my surprise, he doesn't call me names.

Instead, he just threatens my life.

You have one week. You pay the $100,000 you owe us or you're as good as dead.

We will find you, wherever you are.

You know it and we know it, so don't test us.

. . .

The Perfect Cover

I READ the text holding the phone a little bit away from my face.

I know that time is running out.

I know that something's going to happen.

The only problem is that I don't know what that is.

I thought that running away was going to be enough, but now I'm not so sure.

6

TYLER

WHEN I SEE THE THREATS...

The following morning, I wake up early and watch her sleep soundly in bed next to me. Isabelle's shoulders move up slightly with each breath.

I want to stay in this moment for as long as possible, even though I know that's impossible.

Her phone is laying near my pillow in between both of us and suddenly the screen blinks and I see the notifications.

The texts appear on the screen just long enough for me to read without needing her to log in.

The words are visceral and violent, but the intention is clear.

If she doesn't pay up, then they're going to kill her.

They're going to find her wherever she is and they're going to make her pay.

Who are they?

"What are you doing with my phone?" Isabelle asks, sitting up and rubbing her eyes.

"Who are these people?" I ask, turning the phone toward her. "They've been threatening you for a while."

"No, they haven't," she says defensively.

I shake my head and say, "Isabelle, I have to know what's going on. If we are in this together, we have to be honest with each other."

"Why are you going through my phone?" she asks, deliberately avoiding my question.

I shake my head and get out of bed.

I go to the sink, splash some water on my face, and brush my teeth.

If she doesn't want to tell me the truth, then I'm not going to take this any further.

I'm not going to make any threats, but I can't continue to travel with someone who isn't one hundred percent honest with me.

As I stand here, staring at my reflection in

the mirror, with a mouthful of toothpaste, I wonder if I should say these words out loud. I don't want to get into another fight, even though I wouldn't say no to some explosive morning sex, but we have to be on our way.

"Okay," she says, walking up to me. "There is something you should know."

"What?"

"You shouldn't have looked at my phone." She stalls again.

"Maybe not," I agree and wait.

After inhaling deeply, she picks at her cuticles and then looks into my eyes.

"I owe a debt," she finally says.

"What kind of debt?"

"Monetary kind. What other kind is there?" she asks sarcastically.

"Isabelle, if someone is after you, then you have to tell me about it."

She shakes her head.

"I have the right to know."

Again, she shakes her head.

"The federal marshals are after me," I say as calmly as possible, looking straight into her eyes. "Do you know what that means? The power of the federal government is bearing down on *me*, on *us*. They are looking for me and they will do anything to find me. If there is someone else who knows where *you* are and they have something against you, then the feds are going to use that to find me."

"You don't have to worry about it," she says quietly.

"I have to at least know what we're dealing with so that I'm not making decisions in the dark."

I wait for her to tell me but again she bottles herself up.

"It's fine. I'll take care of it."

Now it's my turn to shake my head.

"You have been getting these texts since I was at your house. I have seen some of the threats. Now, they are threatening your life in a very real way. It's not just about me. It's about you. I need to know who these people are and what debt you owe them so that we can make some sort of amends."

I keep repeating myself over and over again, but nothing I say seems to be getting through. Again, she refuses to say a word.

I help her pack up the groceries that she

The Perfect Cover

bought last night and place the last half of a sandwich into the brown paper bag.

"I have money. I'm going to help you pay off this debt."

"You don't have enough," she says without pausing for a moment.

"I have more than you think."

WHEN WE GET BACK into the car and listen to a good hour of Joan Baez and Janice Joplin, I decide to tell her more about myself.

"At the time of my conviction, I had millions in the bank."

"You did?" she asks, surprised.

Turning her body a quarter of the way over to face me in the passenger seat, she waits for me to continue.

"My hedge fund was doing incredibly well. Not only did the fund itself have millions of dollars, but my personal wealth had also grown to almost ten million. I didn't spend it on anything. After I paid off my student loans and bought a few properties, I kept the rest in a bank account. I was a workaholic who didn't do anything but work so my money just grew and grew. My wife spent some of it, but we had so much that she hardly made a dent. In fact, at the time of her death, she was getting into philanthropic causes because there were certain things that we both cared about that we wanted to help raise money for."

"So, what happened?" Isabelle asks.

"What happened was that I got convicted of her murder and they froze all of my assets. The government kept all the money, cash, and sold off the homes as well as liquidated stocks and bonds and other assets. The thing that they did not know, otherwise they would've probably taken that as well, was that I also had a silent partner."

A large tractor trailer passes me on the left and, out of the corner of my eye, I see Isabelle raise her eyebrows.

"She was someone I knew who was, well, let's say not always on the right side of the law. When we were first getting started, she had cash and we needed cash. So, she became a silent partner. She couldn't have been involved for real, on paper, because she had a criminal record and then we wouldn't be able to get the proper licensing for the brokerage, but that was fine by her."

"Silent partner?" Isabelle asks.

"After our investment firm paid back her initial investment plus all the interest," I continue, "she actually borrowed some additional money to expand her own line of business."

"What do you mean?" she asks, narrowing her eyes. Isabelle has always had a good bullshit meter.

"Well, as you might suspect, Tessa's business wasn't exactly on the up and up so she couldn't go to the bank."

She crosses her arms across her chest and waits for me to continue.

"Tessa is in the methamphetamine business. She manufactures it."

"She's a drug dealer?" Isabelle asks.

"More than that." I nod and continue to explain. "When she borrowed money from us, she wanted to expand her operation. She hired a number of chemists, most of them were people who were very good at what they did but felt like they couldn't make enough money working in labs and being teachers.

They had PhDs and would make maybe $60,000 a year. Working for her, they made half a million. When Tessa and I first met, she made all the meth herself, but then she hired two other chemists to help her along. By the time she borrowed money from us and we substantially invested in her business, she had fifty other chemists all across the country. They are all small operations. There are no large meth labs that can be busted. Everyone is a sole proprietor. They make small batches and if they were to get caught and offered a deal by the cops, they wouldn't know who to report on."

"Wow," Isabelle says. "That's pretty brilliant. I always thought that there was one large kingpin somewhere operating these huge labs."

"You're right about one thing, there is a kingpin. It's Tessa. I don't think I have to tell you this, but you can't tell anyone. Not ever. She's a friend of mine, but she won't be if *she knows* that you know."

"Why are you telling me?"

"I'm trying to get you to trust me. I don't

know how much it's going to take, but it seems to require everything I've got."

She swallows hard and turns to look at me again.

"It's not that I don't trust you," she says.

Exhaling slowly, she plays with the ring on her finger before looking up at me again.

"I owe $100,000," Isabelle says after a long pause. She admits something I already know, but this is good. It's the first step.

"Well, good, because Tessa still owes me $300,000."

"What are you talking about?"

"After I went away, there were certain debts that were still unpaid. Of course, she couldn't pay me much while I was in prison—"

"Why?" she asks, interrupting me.

"The authorities would've taken it all. She was sending me some cash here and there for the commissary and what not, but that was all we could manage. She doesn't have too much pull on the east coast, but she also did what she could to make sure that I was somewhat protected on the inside. That also cost a little bit from my end, but if I pay your debt of

$100,000, then I'll still have the two hundred and that's more than enough."

"More than enough for what?"

"To start a new life, to get a new identity, to set up a way to make a living, and finally to hire a private investigator to find out what the fuck happened to my wife and her lover. Then hopefully clear my name."

We don't say anything for a while as I let her stew on the story that I have just given her and take it all in. I know that is a lot.

I didn't think I was going to share this with anyone for a long time, if ever, but the truth is that she has to know.

"So, is this where we're going? To get the money?"

I give her a slight nod.

"Where is that?"

"Palm Desert, California."

"What's the plan? Do you just show up? What makes you think that she won't call the police?"

"Why would she?"

"You do have the $100,000 reward on your head, for one."

The Perfect Cover

I shake my head and give her a slight smile.

"This woman makes millions," I say quietly. "She's very meticulous, organized, and trustworthy. There are not that many people who know what she really is or what she does or what she is capable of. She likes it that way. She will pay my debt because she already paid some of it even when I was in prison, even when I was locked up and completely incapable of enforcing any sort of contract. Verbal or not."

"So, do you think $200,000 is enough to start a new life?" she asks.

"People do it with a lot less all the time."

"Not people in your situation."

"In that case, we'll just have to try and see what happens," I say and turn up the radio.

7

ISABELLE

WHEN HE TELLS ME WHERE WE'RE GOING...

I'm not sure what to think about all the stuff that he just dumped on me. That's not the right way to put it, but I can't think of a better way.

He couched it as if he's telling me the truth, and he probably is, but now I feel like I have no choice but to tell him about my debt.

I never asked him for any of the details about his silent partner, Tessa. In fact, knowing them makes me feel uncomfortable.

It's like our lives are becoming a lot more intertwined than they should be. What is it that happens to people in movies when they see the faces of their assailants? And what happens when they are told secrets they have no business knowing?

I didn't want to know about any of that. Of course, I was curious but I didn't actually want to know.

Now I have to drive the rest of the way knowing that I'm about to meet a woman who grew a methamphetamine empire from nothing to something that's worth millions. You don't do that without a few casualties along the way.

"Why did you tell me that?" I ask, feeling like my heart is about to explode from my chest.

"What are you talking about?" Tyler asks, turning to me as if nothing has happened.

"I didn't want to know any of that. I didn't want to tell you about my debt in order to protect you and now here you are just dumping all of this shit in my lap."

Perhaps, I don't have a reason to be angry.

I'm already traveling with an escaped convict.

I'm already fucked if a cop stops us.

"Why are you mad at me?" he asks.

"How can I not be? I never asked to know any of that and now I can't undo it."

"You can just forget it if you don't want to know," he says.

"You knew exactly what you were doing," I say after a long pause. "You're trying to manipulate me. You're giving me something private. Something that's going to make me trust you. Well, guess what? I already fucking trust you. You don't need to prove anything to me."

"No, you don't trust me," he says. "You know how I know?"

I don't say anything for a moment.

"If you did trust me, then I wouldn't have had to share that secret in order to get you to open up and tell me about your debt. Whatever it is, it can't be as awful as having a meth king as a silent partner in my legitimate business."

I shake my head.

I'm not going to fall for this.

"Is that the whole reason you told me?" I ask.

He stares at me, shaking his head.

"You only told me that to gain my trust?"

We drive in silence for a while, neither of us saying a thing. I'm not just angry but also pissed off.

He says that he just wanted to tell me about Tessa but we both know that's not true.

He wants something from me.

Something I'm not willing to share.

Not yet.

Perhaps, not ever.

ONE HOUR PASSES, and then another. Cornfields whiz by and the sky gets bigger, but not brighter. We are in the heart of the Midwest, where gray clouds hang so low that they almost grace the ground.

I force myself to put my anger away, tuck it into some far away spot, and stare out at the empty black fields rolling by.

I used to be afraid of driving at night. I used to be afraid of driving, in general. In fact, my anxiety was so strong at times that I couldn't force myself to leave the house.

I'm not sure what happened when Tyler showed up. His presence seems to be stronger than any drug that I have ever taken.

Of course, I'm over my anxieties, but they seem to be put on the back burner somewhere, currently unreachable. I wonder why.

Is it because I have other things to worry about?

Before Tyler came into my life, my days consisted of going to work, teaching kids to talk, and then spending my off time obsessing about my worries and insecurities.

And now, on the run from the police, all of that small stuff that I spent my evenings obsessing about doesn't seem to matter.

Is this what it's like for others? I have no idea. But since Tyler has come into my life, things have changed drastically.

Tyler's situation is so complicated and full of actual life and death stakes that it somehow puts everything about me and my worries into perspective. I used to hate going shopping in big department stores and engaging in small talk with the cashiers. I used to hate to drive at night but being here with him has made those concerns dissipate.

Of course, I can't tell my therapist any of this. I have a meeting coming up that I really shouldn't cancel, but I want to, because then I will have to explain what happened to me and what I'm doing on the road.

My therapist is well aware of my situation and how difficult certain things have been for me so, to come forward and tell her how I actually feel and what I'm actually doing, seems like an impossible situation. Especially, since I can't really tell her the truth.

I glance over at Tyler occasionally as he skips a few annoying songs and then settles back into his seat when a good one pops up. I don't really agree with his choice of music, mine goes for something a lot more acoustic, but for now, I let him play it.

I'm still angry at him. Pissed off, actually. He should have never tried to manipulate me into telling him something that I'm not willing to share.

Despite all of that, I can't help but feel safe. For some inexplicable crazy reason, I have felt safer on this road trip, traveling with a convicted felon, than I have in a really long time.

I have no proof about whether or not he's a convicted murderer and perhaps I shouldn't trust my gut in believing that he's not. But I do. I have always relied on my intuition and right now seems like as good a time as any to just go with it.

8

ISABELLE

WHEN WE TALK ABOUT HIS CASE...

When we stop to get gas, Tyler insists on getting it.

I shake my head no.

"We had agreed that I would be the one to pump the gas," I remind him.

He shrugs, turns off the engine, and grabs the door handle.

I put my hand on his leg and he turns to look at me.

"No," I say. "We agreed to certain things to keep you safe and away from the cameras. We have to abide by those rules."

He grips the steering wheel and stares into space.

"If you don't want to be here—" he starts to say, but I put my index finger to his lips.

"Absolutely not," I say quickly. "I want to be here. There are just certain things about you that make me mad as hell, but that doesn't change anything else about our situation."

I wait for him to protest again, but he doesn't. I reach for the door handle and get out of the car. I let out a small sigh of relief when I realize that he's not following me.

I pump the gas until it's full. After getting my credit card back, I place it back into my wallet and get back inside.

We drive miles and miles, getting further and further away from Pennsylvania. The rolling hills of the land back home turn into flat lands that go on for miles into the horizon where the giant sky meets the earth.

Neither of us apologizes and instead, we try to move on. For now, it's the best we can do.

I tell him about the defense attorney that I've read about and then I look up his podcast. I'm not sure about the circulation or how many listeners he has on a weekly basis, but as a fan of true crime, I know that this one is pretty good.

Mallory Deals' voice is smooth, calm, and determined. There's a little bit of arrogance, but not much. Instead, he focuses on the facts.

There are only three episodes, forty-five minutes each, and each one goes into a different part of the trial.

There are no audio recordings from court, but there is a trial transcript that someone reads aloud. Big chunks of it appear in the third episode when Tyler makes me turn it off.

"He's on your side," I say. "He thinks that you have been railroaded."

"I know," Tyler says, giving me a nod, keeping his eyes fixed on the road. "I just can't hear all that again."

"About what he said? About how there's no DNA evidence?"

"There isn't as far as I know," Tyler says. "But I hope that maybe they secretly have some that just hasn't tested."

"How could they have had a trial without evidence?"

"I don't know," he says, shaking his head. "But it has been known to happen. Sometimes the sample is degraded or they will use up too much of it without getting a good sample. At least that's what used to happen in the 90s and the early 2000s."

"Well, it's 2019," I say. "That can't be the case anymore."

He shrugs his shoulders and stares straight ahead.

I'm about to say something else when he stops me.

"I don't want to talk about this," Tyler says. His voice is full of defeat and exasperation.

"You haven't talked about it much." I point out. "I thought that given how long this road trip will take, I could at least get to know some of the details."

"If you want to know the details," he says, whipping his head toward mine, "then read the trial transcript or listen to this podcast on your own. I was there. I have no interest in reliving all the shit that they have said about me."

"I'm not asking you to do that," I say, pleading. "I just need to…"

My voice trails off because I'm afraid of finishing the sentence.

"You need what?" he asks. He narrows his eyes and waits for me to answer.

"I need to understand. I need to know the truth," I say after a long pause.

"You already know the truth."

He clicks back to the CD input and turns up Led Zeppelin.

Disappointed, I put in my earbuds. If he doesn't want to talk about this, that's not going to stop me from learning more about what happened.

As I listen to Mallory Deals' steadfast and relaxed manner of speaking, he starts to lull me into a state of relaxation. His voice isn't boring, per se, just soothing. Honestly, he could be the narrator of one of those sleep podcasts.

I've always enjoyed listening to true crime and watching shows like Dateline and 20/20. This podcast is no different, except that every twenty minutes or so, I have to force myself to remember that the story of this crime, the villain, according to the prosecution, is sitting right next to me.

There are certain facts that the defense attorney confirms. There is no DNA evidence linking Tyler to the crime, but there is also no other DNA evidence linking anyone else to the crime. Sarah and Greg were killed at eleven o'clock at night. Tyler came home around 11:30 that night and called the police. The time of death was an approximation but Tyler's call to the police wasn't.

Despite all of the advances in forensic science, the rate at which bodies decompose, the precise time of the murders was difficult to pinpoint.

There are so many variables that affect the accuracy of the results. For instance, the temperature of the house plays a huge role. If it's hot, the bodies will decompose faster. Blood will coagulate differently when it's warm and humid than when it's cold or chilly. Actually, I'm not sure about the humid part since Deals doesn't exactly mention that.

The authorities said they were killed at 11 PM, but in reality, time of death estimates are just that; estimates. It was sometime that evening, within the last three hours before Tyler showed up. There was also no proof as to when exactly he came home. The neighbor's Nest video camera wasn't working and their other security camera had been off for weeks. It doesn't mean that there was anything suspicious about that except for, of course, it might be.

The podcast does have a recording of the audio that Tyler gave to the police from that night. It was played in court and I hear his voice loud and clear.

Mallory does not shy away from letting the recording run for a long time. I listen to the urgency of Tyler's voice and the panic that set in when he was told that his wife was not only killed but also pregnant at the time of her death.

He gasped and broke down in shock. I remember hearing somewhere that it's easier to tell whether someone is lying not by watching them, but by listening. The truth lies in the audio.

Without the video of Tyler on the stand, and by just listening to his testimony, I am certain that he was either the best actor in the world or a man who was just told that his wife had been murdered, along with, possibly, his unborn child.

Later, tests confirmed that the child was in fact *not* his, but it doesn't make the crimes any less horrendous.

"You wrote Greg an email and threatened him," I say, taking the earbuds out of my ears.

9

ISABELLE

WHEN WE GET THERE...

"So, you got to that part, huh?" Tyler asks.

"Well, didn't you?"

"Yeah, I did. I never denied it. It was a week before or so. Greg had taken my whole business away from me. He stole millions of dollars. I threatened him with legal action, but I also threatened to kill him unless he gave it all back. I should not have done it. I was angry but if I had known it would land me in prison…"

I turn the phone volume up and click back ten seconds to play the recording again.

Someone in court reads from Tyler's email, "You better have the fucking money for me by Monday. If you don't, then you're a dead man. You get that? You're fucking dead and buried."

"You didn't mention any legal action there," I say quietly.

"I did in an earlier email. Actually, I wrote him about seven others before that. He hadn't been returning my calls. He hadn't returned any of my texts or emails. When I wrote that, I found out the extent of the theft and I'd had enough. The next thing I did was place a call to an attorney and send him all of the details about our business. I didn't want to do that. It was a complicated matter and it was going to cost me hundreds of thousands of dollars to defend it in court. I just wanted Greg to pay me my money so we could go our separate ways."

"That didn't happen," I say quietly.

"No, it didn't. Listen, I know that you want to know all of the gory details and maybe you should."

"You don't think I'm entitled to know the truth?" I ask.

"Of course you are, and I want you to ask me questions, but the thing is that I can't listen to it with you. I just can't relive that whole trial minute by minute on that podcast. Even if that guy is on my side. So, why don't you listen to it and if you have questions, you ask me. I'm here. I just can't go through it again."

I give him a slight nod.

I try to imagine what it would be like if I were in his situation.

A part of me thinks that I would want to yell from the rooftops to anyone who would listen so they would believe me. Then I remind myself that Tyler has been going through this for over two years and that's after he had been convicted.

He has been trying to convince people of his innocence for almost four years.

No one has believed him.

Not the cops, not the prosecutor, not the journalists.

His friends all left him.

His first defense attorney ostensibly believed him, but listening to the trial transcript, I now have my doubts.

Actually, it seems to me that the only people that Tyler has on his side are Mallory

Deals and me. Are we delusional or is everyone wrong?

I decide to give Tyler his space. Instead of asking questions as they pop up while I listen, I jot them down on a piece of paper in my journal along with the time code on the screen. This way I'll be able to refer to it quickly in case there's something that he needs to hear.

By the end of the day, when we reach Hannibal, Missouri, I already have five pages of questions and notes.

I'm almost through all of the segments, but there are still a few left.

"How long do you want to drive today?" I ask.

"It depends," he says.

"On what?" I ask.

"Whether the guy that I'm supposed to meet here will show up."

My mouth drops open as I turn to look at him.

"What are you talking about?" I ask. "Are you meeting up with someone?"

He nods.

I shake my head, saying, "It's a trap.

The Perfect Cover

Whoever this person is, they're going to call the cops. There's a warrant for your arrest. Why haven't you told me about this?"

"Don't worry," he says calmly. "I don't even think that he's going to be here."

"Who is *he*?" I ask with my heart racing.

I put my hand over my chest and feel its thumping through my skin.

My breaths quicken and I clench my fist in anticipation.

I watch as Tyler pulls into the center of an old town. We drive past a mural celebrating the life of Mark Twain with depictions of Tom Sawyer and Huckleberry Finn embracing one another.

It's evening, just after twilight and there's no one out. The main street is shut down and all of the stores have CLOSED signs on their doors.

I wonder if this town went by the wayside like so many other small American towns did in the nineties when they opened flag ship plazas in the suburbs, anchored by Walmart and other big box stores.

Tyler's actions are deliberate and focused. It's almost as if he knows exactly where he's going even though I don't know if he has ever been here before.

I keep asking him what's going on over and over again, but it's all to no avail. He doesn't say a thing.

"This is a trap, Tyler. Whoever this is, they're going to call the police. You can't trust him."

He turns to face me.

"I trust him," he says with a smile.

"What are the chances that this other person is as trustworthy?" I ask.

"I don't know if he's going to be here. Don't worry."

"How can you tell me *not* to worry? I don't even know what we're doing here."

He goes down a main street and then pulls off to one of the side streets. The few people that are walking down the street, he watches very carefully, leaning over the steering wheel. Then he pulls into a parking lot and parks the car.

I don't know what to do to make him keep driving. I want to get out, but I'm afraid of the repercussions. I want to make him go, but I know that I can't.

The Perfect Cover

He looks at the time on the clock and waits. His face has a serene quality to it, the kind of expression I haven't seen before. It's almost as if he knows that whether this person is here or not, it's going to be all right.

I am not as sure.

"I can't wait any longer," I say, grabbing for the door handle and unlocking the door.

Before I can free myself, he presses a button and locks me in.

"No," he says sternly. "We have to wait."

10

TYLER

WHEN WE WAIT...

I can remember distinctly when we made the deal to meet here. We picked a date and a time and that was going to be our only shot.

We were sitting together in the cafeteria, having lunch, talking in hushed tones. No one knew that two days from then we were going to attempt the impossible; escape from a maximum-security prison.

There were three of us there and I'm not sure that any of us understood the gravity of the situation.

I know that Lester won't meet us here, but what about Mac?

I don't know where he is.

I don't even have the faintest idea.

The only thing that I am sure about is that he won't betray me.

I glance over at Isabelle and I see the tears in her eyes. She thinks that this is all over while I know that this is just the beginning.

Mac is the only person who I know for sure won't turn me in for the reward money.

Well, Mac and Tessa.

I have never been to Hannibal, Missouri, but it's smack in the middle of the country and on the way to California.

I read many Mark Twain books as a kid and Mac did as well and I was the one who suggested that we should meet up here. Whether that was possible, I had no idea. We decided to give each other ten days to get here.

Traveling with Isabelle and Mac is probably not a good idea, but I owe him and I made a promise.

Hannibal, Missouri, is dressed up like a pageant girl. It's a town with little industry and with only one claim to fame; the birthplace of Mark Twain. That's not a bad claim to fame, actually, most towns don't even have that.

The Perfect Cover

To draw in tourists, they have his childhood home as a museum as well as a few other cultural points of interest. I look for a mural called "Tom Sawyer's Fence."

It's ostensibly the place where the fictional Tom Sawyer character got his friends to whitewash his fence for him, instead of doing it himself like his Aunt Polly told him to.

Mac, Lester, and I had agreed to meet here today at five in the evening. It's 5:30 p.m. and I start to wonder how long I should stay.

I see Isabelle getting antsy, so I turn to face her and tell her what's going on.

She listens carefully, nodding her head, and then exhales slowly.

"You don't think it's a good idea?" I ask.

"No, absolutely not."

"He was my best friend in prison. I wouldn't be here if it weren't for him. We decided to meet to give ourselves a chance to reconnect. I don't know how else to put it, but it feels like we have been through a war and he's the only one that really understands what it was like in there."

"I know that," she says, leaning toward me. "Don't you think I know that?"

I shake my head and say, "If he's here, he won't betray me."

She isn't as convinced.

"I know that you trust him. I know that you two escaped together, but he's not like you, Tyler. He's a murderer."

"You don't know anything about him," I say, turning the radio up.

I don't know how long I should wait, but I want to give him more time. Maybe an hour.

I don't think that he will betray me, but he may not be able to get here on time. Perhaps he's way past this place, somewhere further out west or maybe even in Mexico. After all, he didn't get hurt during our escape and he didn't spend a weekend in Pennsylvania.

"Tyler, you were supposed to meet at five, and it's almost six. Can we just go?"

I should take her up on it, but something tells me to stay put.

"This could be a trap," she says again.

Her distrust is making me angry. I narrow my eyes and glare at her.

"I know that you don't believe me and that you trust him," she says, "but what if he got caught and what if he made a deal?"

I won't admit it but *that* has never occurred to me.

"What if they caught him and what if his attorney got him leniency based solely on information leading to your arrest? They would much rather have two of you than one, no matter what kind of deal they make with the first one."

Blood starts to drain away from my face.

I lick my lips.

They are so parched that I can feel the flakes with the tip of my tongue.

I clear my throat and when that's not enough, I take a swig from the bottle of water in the cupholder.

"You hadn't thought about this," she says, sitting back in her seat. "I can't believe that you hadn't considered this."

"Okay," I say, exhaling slowly.

I don't want to admit that she's right, so I just start the engine. "Let's go."

"Hey there." Mac's voice comes in crystal clear through the crack in my window. "Wait for me."

11

ISABELLE

WHEN WE GET TO OKLAHOMA...

When Mac climbs into the car, the first thing that I notice is his casual, happy-go-lucky smile. He has big white teeth and dusty blonde hair that falls in his face.

He doesn't look anything like a person who has just been on the run for ten days. While Tyler looks tired and detached, even like a deer in the headlights at times, Mac has an easy-going quality to him that's quite attractive.

I get out of the front seat to let him in to the back and immediately he throws his arms around Tyler, giving him a big warm hug.

"Let's get the fuck out of here," he says,

spreading out and taking over the entire back seat.

It's not a big space, it is a Honda Accord after all. I wonder if I should sit in the back and let the two of them reconnect upfront.

"You made it," Mac says, grabbing Tyler's arm again as he drives. "We *fucking* made it."

Mac spreads his arms out over the backs of our seats, sticking his head in between ours.

It's a little bit claustrophobic, but there's not much I can do about it.

As we drive out of town, I look around and check for police cars. I don't think I let out a full sigh until we get back onto the interstate.

"I can't believe you actually came here," Mac says, patting Tyler on his shoulder.

"I can't believe I did either."

"Hell, I thought that this was going to be a set-up for sure."

"So did she," Tyler says, giving me a wink.

There isn't an ounce of cruelty in that wink, just an acknowledgment of the truth.

"I'm sorry," I say shyly.

"Hell, don't be." Mac shakes his head. "I would've thought the same thing. In fact, I did.

This whole way here I kept looking over my shoulder checking to see if there were any cops on the horizon. Of course, if they were, they would have stayed hidden until we connected, but that didn't stop me from looking."

I let out a sigh of relief as we exchange smiles. Now, I don't feel like such a traitor.

"Listen, I wasn't sure you would be here. I wasn't even sure I'd be able to make it here, but, man, it's so good to see you." He throws his arms around Tyler again. Tyler grabs back at him, steering with his knee.

The easiness of their friendship immediately puts me at ease. Perhaps, Tyler was right all along. I should have trusted him.

As we drive through Missouri, darkness falls. It's almost time to pull over, but Tyler wants to make it to Oklahoma. The further west we go and the more states that we put in between us and Pennsylvania, the better off we'll be.

I know this, but my eyelids don't. They start to feel heavier and heavier with each passing moment.

Eventually, I stop fighting it. I simply relax my body and drift off.

I don't wake up again until we get to the Motel 6 parking lot and they tell me that we are at our destination.

I go inside and get a room. They require a credit card and ID. I pray to God that no one is checking on my whereabouts. I don't think they are.

I wouldn't be using the credit card if I had a choice. I have plenty of cash, but the clerk insists.

I want to get two rooms and have some alone time with Tyler, but I know that they have been apart for a long time and have a lot of catching up to do.

Besides, the clerk will definitely remember me and my name if I ask her for two rooms right away. The only way I can figure to do this is to go ahead and get another one sometime later tonight, maybe in a few hours, when there's a shift change. If it's the same clerk, then I can at least explain it by saying that we had a fight.

We have plenty of food in the cooler as well as plenty of snacks, so there's no need to go to the store. Covering their heads with baseball hats and popping their collars up, Tyler and Mac follow me into the room at the far end of the building.

The door goes straight to the outside and faces a big grassy field. The sky is dark as there is no light pollution illuminating and contaminating the view. Somewhere in the distance, I see a swing set with one swing swaying in the wind.

After downing a couple of beers, the guys' mood livens up even more. Their conversation shifts to their escape.

Tyler had gone over some of the details with me, but I'm eager to hear more details from a man who knows how to tell a good story.

"So, how exactly did you get out of prison?" I ask, finishing my can of low carb alcoholic sparkling water and popping open another one.

It has a light raspberry flavor and I like it because it doesn't give me a headache like wine or beer.

"How else do you escape from prison?" Mac asks, leaning back in the plush threadbare maroon chair and propping his feet up on one of the queen-size beds.

"It's a story as old as time. You drill a hole in the wall. You prop up something in your bed so that it looks like someone is sleeping there when the guards make the rounds. You take all of your bedsheets, tie them together, and make your way down the drain."

Mac intertwines his fingers at the back of his head and winks at me as he relaxes in a way that only a free man can.

"Seriously?" I ask. "Just like that?"

I glance over at Tyler who gives me a nod and laughs.

"Despite all of the advances," he says slowly. "Despite all of the technology and all of the things they have set up in that prison, yes, that's the way we did it."

I take a big gulp and let the raspberry liquid wash down my throat.

"I need to know more," I demand, laughing. "Tell me everything."

12

ISABELLE

WHEN WE CONNECT...

I like Mac.

I like him a lot more than I thought I would.

He's fun and easy-going, a lot more than Tyler is. I thought it was just because of Tyler's situation, but now I see that he has a seriousness to him that makes him very different from his friend.

Mac's demeanor puts me at ease. He cracks jokes and laughs in a way that only someone without a care in the world would.

Mac is very different from Tyler and that's a good thing. It's not that I'm tired of Tyler, not even close, but it's nice to travel with someone who isn't so serious all the time. He provides a good amount of comic relief and that's relieving.

"So, tell me more about how you actually did it," I say, opening a candy bar and popping a few pieces into my mouth.

"You know, you're quite interested in this thing, so much so that it's almost suspicious." He glances at me but then starts to laugh and I do as well.

"Hey, I just never met anyone who managed to get out of that situation before."

"Neither have I." Mac laughs.

"Come on," I plead. "Tell me."

"I would've thought that your boyfriend here would've filled you in on the details."

"He said that you used power tools," I admit.

"Oh he did, did he? Did he offer you anymore details?"

I shake my head and glance over to Tyler who stares straight ahead.

"You didn't *tell* her?" Mac asks.

He's genuinely surprised, but I just shrug my shoulders and wait.

"What? What's the big deal?"

"Why did you need power tools?" I ask, trying a different approach.

"To drill through the wall and work our way down through the other walls. They don't make escaping from prison particularly easy nowadays," Mac says with a casual laugh. "We went down a long tunnel and then used the power drills to open up the manhole and climb out."

"Just like that?" I ask.

"Well, it was a little bit more complicated at the time," he admits, "but that was pretty much the gist."

I try to imagine Tyler climbing out of the manhole in the middle of the street.

"Where did the manhole come out to?"

"Just a normal street, nothing too special."

"It was a two-lane highway," Tyler clarifies.

"Oh, shit, of course, I completely forgot."

"Already?" Tyler asks.

"Well, you know me, the details are only moderately important."

As I listen to them banter back and forth, it occurs to me that their differences boil down to this moment; their individual perspectives on the story.

Tyler remembers every detail, worrying and analyzing about every single one. Mac views life from afar. They got out, and damn the details.

Suddenly, I remember something else.

"How did you get the power tools?" I ask again. "Did someone smuggle them in for you?"

Mac looks at me when I turn back. He raises one eyebrow and smiles with the corner of his lips.

"How much do you want to know?" he asks.

I shrug then glance over at Tyler and back at Mac.

"How much are you willing to share?"

"Well, I could tell you that the power tools were just smuggled in through our connections and that's it. Or I could tell you who did the smuggling."

Now I'm intrigued, but I don't get my hopes up.

I hardly know him and I probably shouldn't know this anyway.

The Perfect Cover

Mac glances over at Tyler and waits for him to give him the go-ahead.

"Hey, it's your story. It's up to you whether you want to tell it or not."

"I've got nothing to be ashamed of."

I wait for him to continue. He takes a deep breath and leans closer to me.

He's so close that I smell the minty freshness of his breath from his gum. He makes a small bubble and pops it, showing himself to be an expert at building anticipation.

"I had a thing going with one of the guards."

"Really?" I ask, inching closer to him, awaiting the next bit of juicy gossip.

"Yeah. We had a thing for about a year. He was very shy about it. Some guards aren't. With some, it's basically an open secret."

"Is that allowed?" I ask.

"Which part? Same-sex relationships, relationships with guards, or relationships altogether?"

"I guess any of those. I don't know," I say, confused.

"Smart girl," Mac says with a laugh.

"You're absolutely right. They frown upon all relationships in there, but especially the ones between inmates and guards. I'm not really sure how they feel about same-sex relationships though. Tyler? What do you think?"

Tyler shrugs and glances over at me. "You know that he's fucking with you, right?"

"What do you mean?" I ask. "Did this not happen?"

"No, it did," Tyler says. "Mac just likes to make everything a little game."

"Hey, you would, too, if you were in the slammer for as long as I was."

That sentence strikes me as the most honest thing that Mac has said in my presence up until this point. The reality is that he has been in there for years and that changes people. It can't *not* make an impact.

"Listen, I didn't want to make it this whole serious thing," Mac says. "I was just joking around. The truth is that Lindsey and I had a thing going for a while. I liked him. He was fine and had a dry sense of humor. He also had a wife and four children that were making his time at home quite miserable. I'm not sure whether there was anything really wrong with his family, but I think that they were just wrong for him."

"Oh, I'm sorry," I mumble.

"Don't be," Mac says. "Really, it's a tale as old as time. He refused to acknowledge himself as he really was so he went overboard trying to live this perfect little suburban life, with a hefty mortgage and too many obligations. I'm not saying that four kids is too many, just that they were too many for *him*. Frankly, I don't think Lindsey had the energy to deal even with one."

"So, no one knew about you two?" I ask.

"Tyler and Lester did, but not many others."

"So, did Lindsey help you get out?"

"He wasn't fully aware of the plan," Mac says, "but when I asked him for the power tools, he got them for me. Take that as you may."

"So, what do you think is going on now?"

"What do you mean?" Tyler asks me.

"Well, with your escape, do you think people are interrogating him? Like the cops or the FBI?"

"It's a strong possibility," Mac says, "but I haven't heard anything about anyone helping us escape. I don't think Lindsey will go and volunteer that information because he was pretty much of an in the closet kind of a guy as I've ever met. If his wife had walked in on us having sex, he'd deny it."

I go through my phone and search for any articles that mention a guard, Lindsey Broker, or power tools, but nothing comes up. I check the message boards as well, but again I see nothing.

"There isn't anything?" Mac asks, glancing over my shoulder.

I shake my head no.

"Good," he says, sitting back with a satisfied expression on his face. "That's a surprise, but a good one. I guess Lindsey is better at keeping secrets than I thought he would be."

13

ISABELLE

WHEN WE GET SOME ALONE TIME...

I like Mac, but despite that, I want some alone time with Tyler. I feel like I usually do and probably like so many other people do in the beginning of relationships, when they really can't get enough of each other. Only our situation is vastly more complicated, made only stranger by the fact that we are now traveling with a fellow felon.

When Mac zones out in front of the television and his eyelids begin to grow heavy, I pull Tyler to the side and motion to him.

"What's wrong?" Tyler asks.

"Nothing," I say when we close the door behind us. I take his hand in mine.

He holds my hand tightly and we wander into the cornfield, following a path laid by an inconsiderate ATV user.

"I know that Mac can be a lot to handle," Tyler says. "So, I just wanted to thank you for being so welcoming."

"Yes, of course," I say quickly. "I actually like him."

"I know, but you'll see what I mean in a little bit."

I crunch my eyebrows together, unsure as to how to take this information in.

We walk toward the swing set and Tyler offers it to me since there's only one. I haven't sat in a swing in years.

The weightlessness is intoxicating. I swing lightly and then lift up my feet as Tyler stands slightly behind me and gives me a light push every time I come back to him.

"So, what's the deal with Mac?"

"What do you mean?"

"Earlier he talked about his girlfriends and then he had the thing with the guard. Is he bi?"

Tyler laughs, shaking his head, and then

says, "I don't think he identifies as any group in particular. I would just say that he is a very, very sexual being."

"That's cool," I say absentmindedly.

Tyler shrugs, giving me another push.

"Things are very simple in prison. There are no women except for a few guards and the vast majority of them take their jobs very seriously."

"What does that mean?"

"Any sort of sexual relationships are against the rules and most guards abide by that. That pretty much leaves us inmates to our own devices. Or vices."

I give him a nod and ask, "What about you? Have you ever been with... A man?"

"No," Tyler says, "but that doesn't mean that it wouldn't have happened if I had been in there as long as Mac."

There's a frankness to his voice, a calmness actually. There's no judgment, in fact there is just acceptance of the way things are.

The sky is blue, that sort of thing.

I appreciate the candor and the honesty.

I continue to swing and we don't say

anything for a long time. It's just nice to be here all alone surrounded by only fireflies and birds.

"What did Mac do to get life in prison?" I ask.

"Sold drugs. He got caught with pounds of cocaine, I can't remember exactly how much, but he had been a big trafficker. He killed someone from a rival gang and the judge threw the book at him."

"How long has he been in there?" I ask.

"Seven years. A day in there is like two months on the outside, just for perspective."

I nod and shuffle my feet.

"I should've told you about him earlier and our pact about meeting up. I know that was a surprise for you and I really shouldn't have sprung it on you."

I turn around in my swing and face him. He kneels down pulling me closer into his arms.

"I had to keep that promise to Mac about meeting up even if it was futile, even if there was a possibility of him setting me up. It was a distant possibility, but I guess it was a possibility."

"Okay," I say slowly, internalizing what he is saying to me.

"Mac saved my life in prison. These two guys, big beefy ones, kind of like the ones they always show on all those prison shows, attacked me in the shower. They tried to rape me. They would have if it weren't for Mac. He fought them off. Everyone in there was divided into factions. I didn't really have one. I was what they called unaffiliated. Those guys saw that as a weakness and they tried to take something from me. Mac fought them off, putting a mark on his head. We had only been friends for a couple of weeks leading up to that and I wasn't expecting him to do anything close to that to help me. The fact that he did…" Tyler's voice trails off, still for the appreciation of what his friend did for him.

I wrap my arms around him and hold him tightly.

"I'm so sorry that you went through all of that," I say. "I wish there was something I could do to help."

"You are already doing it," Tyler says, pulling away from me. There's a small tear forming in the corner of his eye, but he wipes it off before it has a chance to roll down his cheek.

14

ISABELLE

WHEN I HAVE A MEETING...

The following day, we stop driving at noon and pull over to a diner to get some food and some gas. It's a little out-of-the-way place and it's in a dusty little town. I'm nervous about having the guys eat there, but Mac keeps insisting.

"It's going to be fine," he says. "You'll see."

"Why even take the chance?" I ask as Tyler cuts the engine. "We have enough food here. We can stop at a rest stop and have a sandwich. We can even get some drive-thru. I just don't see the point of going inside an establishment."

I glance over at Tyler and wait for him to

agree with me. Much to my surprise he doesn't.

"It's going to be fine, Isabelle," he says, optimistically.

After Mac gets out of the car, I reach over and take Tyler by the arm.

"Why are you doing this?" I ask in a low quiet voice. "Why take an unnecessary risk? What if someone recognizes you?"

"They won't," he insists.

"You have no idea what's going to happen."

I don't know if I'm overreacting, I really hope that I am, but I just don't see the point. It's like wearing a seat belt.

You don't know if you're going to get in a car accident and you probably won't, but why not take the extra precaution, which might save your life?

Tyler, however, refuses to listen to me.

"Are you coming?" he asks, walking to the front door.

I shake my head.

"Are you kidding?"

I shake my head and say, "I have an

appointment anyway but even if I didn't, I still think this is a terrible idea."

"Oh, is that today? With your therapist?"

I nod.

"Can you get out of it?"

"Yes, of course, but it's something that I typically do every week and my life has already been quite predictable . I don't want to draw any more attention to myself than necessary."

"Of course. Well, just come on in when you're done or let me know what you want me to order for you."

Angry and pissed off, I shake my head and say, "I don't want you to order anything for me."

I turn on the heel of my shoe and walk away from him with a huff.

INDIA BROWNSTEIN IS a beautiful woman in her 50s. She has smooth skin, deep black eyes, and dark hair that's illuminated by strands of silver.

She's located in Nantucket and we have

never met in person. I contacted her after I realized that I needed someone to talk to after my last breakup and didn't want to go into an office every week. I feel more comfortable talking online and she has been more than accommodating.

As it turns out, India has clients all over the United States and Canada as well as Dubai, Singapore, and the United Kingdom. She rarely talks about herself, but when I looked her up online, I saw articles about her practice in Nantucket Magazine, LA Magazine, and the New York Times.

I have no idea what prompted her to take me on as a client, but a part of me suspects that she just felt sorry for me. I pay way more than I can really afford and that's about half her usual rate. Over this last year, she has become something of a mother figure to me. My own mother is drastically different and she's completely impossible to speak with.

India is not like that.

She listens.

She understands.

Occasionally, she gives advice, but mainly she asks questions.

Her goal is to help me figure out the right thing to do by not telling me what should or shouldn't be done.

I have opened up to her more than I have opened up to anyone else.

She knows practically everything, all the good and the bad.

Somehow, that's okay.

My phone connects with her computer and I see her face on the screen. There's a quiet and calmness to her that immediately puts me at ease.

She sits close enough to the screen that I can actually see her face, every reaction. I've noticed how important that is when talking to people through teleconference. If people are too far away it feels like you're giving a speech in a room.

It's like they're there but they're not there.

Meanwhile, when they are right next to you, and their face fills up the whole screen of your phone, there's an immediacy and a presence to that experience that is difficult to describe.

"Well, hello there," India says, giving me a slight wave of the hand.

Her new nails are polished, but not overdone, just like the rest of her. Her shoulders are draped in some sort of shawl, embroidered with the pleasant colors of the ocean.

There is a thin necklace around her neck with a little crescent moon that buries itself right in between her collarbones.

The stud earrings, at least a carat each, in each earlobe, make her eyes sparkle.

"Hi," I say nervously, touching my hair and adjusting the way it looks in the little screen.

"How are you? What's new?"

I have emailed her about my trip and she knows the broad strokes. Basically, it's the same story that I told my coworkers.

"Well, I'm on this little road trip. I just decided to take a chance and go."

"That's very unlike you," India says, "but I'm glad to hear it. How is your anxiety?"

"I try not to think about it. I'm not really obsessing about going into the rest areas or in the convenience stores. I've been listening to a lot of music and audiobooks."

"So, what has spurred all of this?" she asks.

She doesn't sound like she's interrogating me, more like she's just curious.

"It's silly actually," I admit. "I watched this movie, *Crossroads*. It's with Britney Spears and it's about twenty years old. It's about three friends who take a road trip together and I sort of felt like if they could do it, then why couldn't I?"

"That's very true. Staying in one place for a long time, especially not having much social contact like you do, outside of work, it can be a little difficult on your mental health. I'm actually very proud of you for taking this initiative."

"I don't think I would've done it if I had given it much thought."

"That's a good thing. For you, anyway. For some people who have problems with impulse control, we try to suggest other coping strategies. For you, I'm glad that you jumped at the chance to embrace this opportunity."

We talk for a little bit more and I feel like my thoughts start to clear.

I stop worrying about what I should or

shouldn't be doing and instead focus on being more intuitive. We make plans to talk again next week and I promise to contact her if I start to feel anxious or out of control again.

"Call me anytime," she says.

"Yes, of course," I say.

"Isabelle, I mean it. Please call me if you start to feel strange or anything unusual. I want this to be a good experience and I hope it pushes you forward and doesn't set you back."

I thank her, hang up the phone, and stare out at the empty parking lot behind the diner.

I have made at least ten loops around here while talking to her but never really looked at it.

The asphalt is worn and tired, beaten down after years of winter storms and summer humidity.

There's another field to the left, stretching far into the distance. The sky is bright blue and entirely cloudless.

There's something very relaxing about being out here. It's almost as if this sky gets very big and stays that way. With the hills and the low hanging clouds back home, it always felt like someone was encroaching on my thoughts.

Watching me.

Bearing down on me.

Perhaps even suffocating me.

Out here, where the Earth is flat and the sky is big enough to swallow up the whole world, I feel the kind of freedom that I haven't felt in a long time.

"So, what did you tell her?" Mac asks.

I spin around as his voice startles me.

"Nothing," I say with a shrug.

I don't like his accusatory question but I decide to let it go.

"We are running away from the FBI and you take half an hour to talk to your therapist?"

"I'm not running away. I didn't tell her anything about you or Tyler. She doesn't even know that I'm here. No one does."

"Are you sure about that?"

"Yes, of course I'm sure. I had the appointment set up before I took the days off work. She knows that I have certain anxieties about traveling. I'm doing everything in my power to make sure that we don't get caught. I *can't* really say the same about you."

He narrows his eyes and smiles out of the corner of his mouth.

"Everything was fine and the food was delicious," he says, mocking me.

"I didn't say that it wouldn't be. There's just a good chance that someone could recognize you both and I don't see the point of taking the risk."

"Well, there was a good chance that we couldn't have gotten away from that prison and now look at us. Free men."

"You won't be free men for long if you keep it up. Your faces are everywhere. There's a big reward for your arrest or capture. You may not care about that, but I care about Tyler and I don't want anything like that happening to him."

"I care about Tyler, too, and I promise you nothing will."

"You can't make that promise. You can promise it, but you can't keep it."

"You know," Mac says, leaning on the car and narrowing his eyes like James Dean, "you would be a lot more fun if you loosened up."

I clench my jaw. That's the kind of thing that men say when you don't agree with them and when they're losing an argument.

When I get back in the car, I don't mention any of this to Tyler.

We drive for hours into Texas. A big part of me wants to bring it up, but the moment passes.

I can't wait to get to the room and to talk to Tyler in private, but then it dawns on me that Mac will probably be there tonight as well.

It's difficult for me to rent two rooms without looking very suspicious but after that little exchange in the parking lot, the last thing I want to do is share a room with him again.

When we stop to get gas that evening, the pump doesn't work and I go inside to pay cash. There's a large television above the clerk's head, with a primetime story about the escapees and the reward.

My heart skips a beat.

Back in the car, Mac refuses to believe it, Tyler does. He then agrees that we need to find a Rite Aid as soon as possible so that I can buy some box color and give them new looks.

That evening, we pull into another Motel 6 with another bored clerk behind plexiglass.

Again, she asks me for my ID and credit card in case there's any damage.

Again, I wonder if all of these charges are going to be bread crumbs for the FBI to find Tyler, Mac, and me.

At this point, I don't think that the story about holding me as a hostage is going to work.

15

ISABELLE

WHEN WE'RE ALONE...

After getting to the motel room and grabbing a bite to eat, I let the guys argue about who should get which color.

I got one box of chestnut color and another in dirty blonde. Both should be pretty natural-looking, but still different from the pictures they have all over television.

I prefer for Tyler to go lighter, but I'm afraid that if I were to voice that opinion, then it wouldn't happen. Instead, I sit back and relax, flip through the channels, and wait to see what happens.

They go back and forth, fighting over the small mirror in the bathroom. They examine each other's hair and then compare. They talk about the models on the boxes and debate which one would look better with which color.

They remind me of twelve-year-old girls examining themselves in the sixth grade bathroom. It really makes my day.

"You're laughing, but this is harder than it looks," Mac says.

He is back to being the easy-going gregarious guy who I was first introduced to.

We haven't talked about India again and for that, I'm thankful.

"Those are the best colors they had. L'Oréal is a good box color. I've used it myself a number of times."

"You have?" Tyler asks. "I thought that women always went to salons."

"Not everyone can afford $200 stylist fees for a color and a cut. That's every six weeks if you're lucky."

He looks concerned and worried about how it's going to turn out.

"It's going to be okay," I reassure him. "You're not going to have green hair."

"I don't want to have orange hair either."

The Perfect Cover

I see that he's leaning toward a lighter shade.

"It's not going to be," I promise.

I know that it's harder to go lighter than it is to go darker. His hair isn't that dark though and the lighter shade isn't that light, so I hope that this will work out.

Eventually, they reach an agreement and Tyler goes with the lighter one and Mac goes with the darker one.

Instead of reading directions, they ask me for help. They want me to do it for them but I'm tired after the long drive and the shopping trip.

I show them the basics and let them use my comb to make parts. They try to put the color in their hair evenly around their head and I check if they missed any spots in the back.

Tyler is careful and meticulous. It takes him twice as long, but the job is even and careful.

Mac is out of control. There are drips all over the sink and the bathmat. When I check his head for spots, I can't see a thing since he had pushed all the hair together and mixed it all up.

They're supposed to keep the color on for thirty minutes and, of course, they don't stagger themselves. When Mac jumps into the shower, Tyler rinses his in the sink and washes off the rest after Mac gets out.

An hour later, after we get takeout from the Denny's next door, I am pleasantly surprised that both of their efforts have worked to their benefit.

Tyler smiles at me through his sandy blonde hair that falls lightly in his face. I give him a wink and glance over at Mac.

"I'm going to have to try this new hair out on the ladies," he announces, brushing his hand through his chestnut brown strands.

"Yeah, maybe when we get to California," Tyler says.

Mac shakes his head.

"You're not thinking of going out tonight?" Tyler asks.

"Of course!"

Tyler frowns and looks to me for support.

"Listen, I know that you're a worry-wart like your girl here, but nothing's going to happen. Besides, we are in some little town that no one has ever heard of. People here probably don't even watch the news."

"Everyone watches America's Most Wanted," I interject.

"No, they don't. Maybe they did in the 90s when there were like three channels, but now with Netflix, Hulu, YouTube, and who knows what else, what are the chances of anyone seeing us?"

"Really good," I press. "Besides, there's a $100,000 bounty on your heads. Who do you think lives in this town that won't turn you in for that kind of money?"

I feel anger rising within me, but it just doesn't feel like Tyler is standing up for his interests well.

Why can't he talk some sense into Mac?

If he doesn't want to, then why the hell are you traveling with him in the first place?

"Listen, guys," Mac says in that casual fun-guy sort of manner that's supposed to put me at ease, but actually does the complete opposite. "This is going to be a dive bar. Dark, dingy, but hopefully still populated with cute girls from town who are eager to get together with a mysterious stranger. I'm going to take every precaution but trust me they're not going to recognize me."

I don't want to argue anymore so I step out for some fresh air.

Part of me wishes I was a smoker so that I could have a good reason for being out here, but I don't.

Instead, I just stare down at my phone and scroll aimlessly through social media, listening to the muffled voices through the door.

I can't make out most of what they're saying, but as the conversation goes on, their voices are getting more and more elevated.

I hear Tyler trying to reason with Mac, giving him all of the same arguments that I presented earlier when we went to the diner.

I also hear Mac responding back that he doesn't think it's a risk. He argues that no one's going to expect to see him here so they won't recognize him even if they had seen the program.

Besides, he now also has a new look, thanks to the new hair color and the trim that I had given him earlier.

Of course, all of these things were

supposed to be precautionary measures, they were supposed to create an order of protection around him, *not* give him a reason to take unnecessary chances.

This doesn't get through to Mac.

The last thing I see when he walks out the front door is him rolling his eyes at Tyler as he disappears down the stairs.

I come back into the room and look at Tyler who is lying on one of the queen-size beds, completely defeated.

His hands are folded tightly behind his head and he is staring straight at the popcorn ceiling.

The heater, next to the only window facing out, rumbles and puts out a puff of heat. I turn it down a little bit, but Tyler tells me not to touch it because it might not come back on.

The room is hot and stifling.

It's March and the ice-cold wind is barreling through every crevice in the door and window.

Since I can't turn down the heat, I just strip down to my T-shirt and even take off my socks.

"I swear I'm going to get a cold from

coming in and out so much," I joke, but only partly. "It's so hot in here and arctic out there. The last thing I need is to get sick."

"You can't get a cold from the cold. You get sick from bacteria or a virus, not the cold," Tyler says, staring at the ceiling and avoiding my gaze.

The tone of his voice is detached and deadpan so it's hard to know if he is serious or just lost in his own thoughts.

"What did Mac say?" I ask.

"That he needed to get laid and that the only reason I was stopping him was because I had someone to lay with."

"Is that why?" I ask.

"No," he says with a sigh. "I mean, I would hope not but I can't fault him. It's been a really long time since he has been with a woman. He's the kind of guy that has always enjoyed that, probably a lot more than the rest of us."

"Still. That's no reason to jeopardize everything that you have worked for. Not just for him, but for you, too."

"I know," Tyler says, sitting up. "I know all of that. I know where you're coming from and

The Perfect Cover

I agree with you, but another part of me sees his position, too. If he were to get caught and not have this night as a free man, just hanging out, grabbing a beer at a bar, flirting with a girl or two, then what's it all for? This could be our last night out here."

"It's *going to be* our last night out here if you keep letting him act like this. First, you both go to the diner and now he's going to a bar. We're all going to get caught."

Tyler looks at me and tilts his head.

"Let me ask you a question," he says slowly. "Are you worried about *us* getting caught or are you worried about *you* getting caught?"

"Both," I say. "Of course, I'm worried about you and to some degree him, but I'm really going out on a limb here. I don't think they're going to believe that you kept me hostage even if we end up going with that story. If they don't, then I'll be facing years in prison. If we get caught because of something so stupid like eating at a diner or going to a bar, what am I doing this for?"

"I don't know why you're doing this, Isabelle. I warned you that you wouldn't want to be here. I told you that it wouldn't be safe."

"No, correction," I say, pointing my finger in his face. "You never told me about Mac. You didn't tell me that we were going to pick up somebody who was so reckless and just out to have a good time. I know that he's your friend and that he saved you in there and that you owe him, but you owe me, too. You should've told me the truth. You shouldn't have kept him a secret. I deserve to know what I'm getting into before I risk my life and freedom to be out here with you."

Tyler glares at me and then leans forward.

I want to push him away but suddenly I feel this magnetic pull toward him.

I want to talk about this.

This conversation isn't over, but when our bodies collide, I know that we're not going to talk about it for a while.

Tyler kisses me.

I am still angry so I kiss him back, hard.

He presses his lips so hard against mine that it almost hurts, but in a good way.

When we pull apart, I bite him. For a moment, he's surprised, narrowing his eyes.

"What do you think you're doing?"

"Whatever the fuck I want," I say, challenging him.

His jaw clenches and his eyes evaluate me. They look me up and down before he opens his mouth.

"Take off your clothes."

It's more of a command than a request and I like that.

"You first," I say, straightening my back and crossing my arms.

Without a moment of hesitation, he pulls off his shirt.

The muscles in his stomach protrude with each breath, flexing and relaxing.

I'm mesmerized by their power.

In addition to the six pack, he even has the V-shaped muscles on the sides leading down to his groin.

His jeans hang low, right at his hipbones making me lick my lips.

"Your turn," he says casually.

I shake my head.

"Do you want me to make you?"

I shake my head but smile at the corner of my lips.

"If you don't do it yourself, I'm going to make you," he threatens, but it's a veiled threat.

He knows that I want this and I know that he wants this as well.

The only thing that's stopping me is the fact that I'm still mad at him.

I take a deep breath and gather my strength.

"No," I say sternly. "We can't do this."

"Why?"

"I'm mad at you. We're not done talking about what happened."

"Since when does *that* matter?" he asks.

I get up and walk away from him but Tyler takes a few steps closer and wraps his arms around my shoulders.

"I love you," he whispers into my ear.

I feel myself melting before him, but I have to remain strong.

"I want you," he whispers.

"I want you, too," I say silently to myself, refusing to let the words escape from my lips.

He presses his lips to the back of my earlobe and kisses me. This time, his lips are soft and effervescent like butterfly kisses.

I turn around to face him and he kisses me hard on the lips.

Suddenly, I can't say no.

I want him so much that I throb for him in my core.

I kiss him back, just as hard.

Our lips are a perfect match. Our tongues intertwine.

The kiss is messy and dirty.

That's just like we want it.

He pushes me toward the bed. We stumble over a chair and a bag, but eventually it catches us.

He pulls down my leggings along with my panties and rubs his fingers between my legs.

I'm wet and I want him.

Tyler unbuckles his jeans and lets them fall to the floor. He presses against me.

I feel the hardness and the largeness of his cock.

We continue to kiss as I wrap my fingers around him and hold onto it like a joystick in a video game.

He digs deeper inside of me with his fingers as I start to slide my hand faster and faster.

"I need to be inside of you," he says.

"Yes," I mumble. "Me, too."

He reaches over and picks up his jeans off the floor, reaching for something in the back pocket. He pulls out a little square and it makes a loud crinkling sound when he opens it to take out the condom.

He slides it on quickly and effortlessly.

Then he carefully slides in me.

I'm not a small girl, by any stretch of the imagination, but the way that he handles me, it makes me feel like Tinker Bell.

He pushes in and out of me quickly, going deeper and deeper each time.

My legs wrap tightly around his torso and he holds himself with his arms, pressing me harder and harder against the bed.

My whole body tightens just as I start to feel that familiar explosion building up.

I moan his name over and over, letting my body go limp as soon as I'm consumed by a wave of pleasure.

16

ISABELLE

IN THE MORNING...

The wind howls outside the whole night and my sleep is restless and uneven.

I wake up every few hours and go to use the bathroom in complete darkness.

I illuminate my way with my phone and the empty bed next to ours does not go unnoticed.

Mac hasn't come back.

When I finally wake up for good around five o'clock from a bird chirping loudly on the railing outside, I stare at the untouched bedspread and a cold sweat runs down my back.

Where is he?

Did something happen?

Did they catch him?

Are they coming for us?

Tyler snores peacefully next to me, completely unbothered by the turn of events.

I'm tempted to wake him, but there is no point in us both worrying. There's not really a point to me worrying either except that I can't stop.

I try to meditate, but when I close my eyes, all I see are police cars surrounding the motel with their lights flashing and their alarms blaring. A gun points in my face and I stare into its long barrel going further and further into the darkness.

This is the end of us.

Is this how my life is going to come to the finish line?

I try to distract myself with my phone.

I read the news and scroll down social media accounts. I put on *The Office* on Netflix, a show that I've seen hundreds of times, but even that doesn't distract me from my own brooding thoughts.

I consider going on a run, but after the heater shut off in the middle of the night, I'm too cold to even climb out from under the covers.

I also think about taking a hot shower, but when I breathe out and see the path of cold air in front of me, I can't bear to force myself to get undressed no matter how hot the water might be.

Suddenly, the door swings open. Mac stumbles in, tripping over a chair and catching himself on the table.

I can smell the booze on his breath from across the room.

"I'm fine, I'm fine," he says in a loud whisper, waking up Tyler.

"You just got back?" Tyler asks, rubbing his eyes. "Shit, it's fucking cold in here."

"Really?" Mac asks, taking off his coat and revealing nothing but a white T-shirt underneath.

In this early morning light, with his newly dark hair swept back, and a cigarette hanging from his mouth, he looks like James Dean.

"The heater broke," I say. "You should probably put your jacket back on."

"So, how did it go?" Tyler asks.

"I'll tell you later," Mac says, plopping

down on the bed. "I just have to get some shut eye for a few minutes."

We don't let him.

Tyler insists on packing up our stuff and leaving as soon as possible. I agree except that I really don't want to climb out of bed. Tyler keeps Mac awake, eventually helping him down to the car and forcing him into the back seat.

"He stayed up all night. He'll probably sleep until the afternoon if we let him. It's better that he does while we're getting hundreds of miles away from this place," Tyler says.

I like how he takes control of the situation. I was getting really tired of being the only reasonable one in this caravan.

After watching him pack all of our bags and carrying them down to the car, I put on my most comfortable leggings with a thick sweatshirt along with two other long sleeve shirts underneath and climb into front passenger seat.

By the time he pulls out of the parking lot, Mac starts to snore and my eyelids get heavy and I drift off.

The Perfect Cover

WE DON'T DRIVE VERY FAR the next day as everyone is feeling quite tired.

I didn't get much sleep and apparently neither did Tyler.

Mac is too hungover to drive for long.

Instead, we stop right on the border of Texas and New Mexico at another one-star motel.

For about two hours leading up to stopping, Tyler and Mac talk about anything and everything; sports, politics, television, movies, and even art.

In case you're wondering, Tyler likes impressionism and modern 20th-century while Mac prefers the Dutch Masters.

Apparently, there was a girl that Mac dated who was an artist and she taught him all about the history of art.

By the time we get to our next destination, I'm getting pretty sick of being the third wheel. Mac and I are actually getting along, joking around a bit, but the car trip is still not going as I had planned.

I thought that this would be a time for

Tyler and me to connect and really get to know each other, but instead I'm sharing the precious time that I have with him with a third-party.

In fact, sometimes it feels like I'm the one tagging on *their* road trip.

We stop by a gas station to get some booze. When we get to the room, I'm not surprised to see another field out back. These motels along the interstate always seem to be surrounded by wide open spaces.

There are a few other motels and hotels along with some diners and fast food restaurants, catering to weary travelers, but that's usually it.

No city.

No town.

Not even a shopping plaza.

There are fewer people out here, but as a result we are also more noticeable. When Tyler suggested that we stay in one of the cities we passed, I shut him down.

I don't have a lot of money to spare and we are already spending seventy bucks a night. A motel that cheap in the city is going to be way worse than the ones along the interstate.

They'll probably even be populated with people who tend to attract police attention and that is the last thing I want, to be caught in the crossfire.

Again, I want it to just be the two of us and, again, I'm stuck sharing a room with both of them.

A part of me wishes that Mac would go away and go drinking again, but another part of me wishes that he would stay put so we can get there as safely as possible.

While it's still light out, I decide to leave them with their beers and go on a walk to clear my head.

"Where are you going to go?" Tyler asks when I grab my purse. "There's just a road, that's it up ahead."

"I don't know. I'm getting a little bit claustrophobic being in the car and then being stuck here in this little room."

They are each three beers in and I wonder if the couple of six packs that we have left is going to be enough.

I want Tyler to follow me, but he doesn't.

I don't wait long.

I don't know how long I can make it out

here in the cold but a part of it feels almost refreshing and relaxing. The wind picks up in the desert but still I go further and further behind the parking lot.

Outside, I admire the beautiful colors of the Southwest. The sky is some sort of majestic color of light blue, fuchsia pink, and little sprays of red. There are a few cacti here and there, sprouting up all covered in flowers.

Spring is supposed to be the most beautiful time in this region and I wish that we were going through the Grand Canyon or Tucson on our way to California.

I have never seen a saguaro cactus in real life and I have only viewed the Grand Canyon on Google. Both seem to be like these magical otherworld beings that only exist in another dimension or perhaps in another life.

When I get tired of walking, I find a little bit of shelter in the curve of the land and kneel behind a puffy shrub of creosote.

I sit down and pull out a yellow notebook. I've always had this dream of one day writing something, but when it came right down to it, I never could.

The truth is that I never really tried, but

The Perfect Cover

India has always encouraged me to put my thoughts on paper and I figure now is as good a time as any.

I consider the fact that if someone finds this journal, then they will probably use it against me, especially if that someone is a law enforcement officer.

So, I don't want to write anything specific. I want to write in metaphors and yet no metaphors come.

I sit for a while staring at the blank piece of paper. The paper is thick with many imperfections. The edges are uneven, almost as if they have been ripped.

The cover itself is made from vegan leather and is about the size of a mass-market paperback. I got it on a whim at a gift store and paid way too much for it. It's one of those beautiful journals that is almost too gorgeous to actually mess up with written words.

I press the pen onto the paper and try to make the first word, but nothing comes.

I'm not a poet.

I'm not someone who can write in metaphors.

I'm not someone who can write one thing

and have it mean another.

Maybe I don't have to.

Something else occurs to me. What if I were to just write and then get rid of the pages? I can get it all out on paper, the truth, and I wouldn't have to worry about anyone finding it.

I turn the first page, hesitate only for a moment, and then begin.

I start from the beginning.

I don't think about the words, I just relay the feelings and everything that happened.

Occasionally, I'm tempted to lie. I'm tempted to write about how Tyler took me hostage and that I'm really here against my will, but that would be fiction and I can't bring myself to do it.

The truth is okay, I tell myself. I won't hang onto these pages for long.

I just need to get it all out.

I write until my hand cramps and my fingers turn to ice.

"Hey!" I yell. Mac snatches the journal from me so suddenly that my pen leaves a thick, black line down the center of the page, evidence of my protest.

"What are you doing?" I gasp.

I reach over to get it back from him but he holds it over my head as if we were back in elementary school.

Whenever I try to reach for it, he keeps turning the pages, reading bits and pieces here and there and shaking his head.

"You can't do this," he says.

I jump up, trying to grab it away from him, but again he eludes me.

He is faster, stronger, and taller than I am and now he's holding one of the most precious things I own.

"You can't write this," Mac says.

"You don't even know what it says, you didn't even read it."

"I can read more if you want," he offers.

"Fuck you," I say, gritting my teeth.

"You can't write this. You're supposed to be a hostage. If anyone finds this, then they'll never believe you."

"I know," I mumble softly.

"Since we have no idea if we will be caught or when, I'm going to do something to protect you against yourself." He grabs the pages and violently rips them out.

I gasp, unable to believe my eyes.

Is this really happening?

"What are you doing?"

He takes out a lighter and starts a flame.

I reach over to stop him.

He jumps away from me and the flame goes out.

"You know I have to do this, Isabelle."

"No, you don't. That's mine."

"Let me ask you a question," he says seriously, looking deep into my eyes. "When the front desk clerks ask you who you're traveling with, you give them fake names. You protect Tyler's identity. You protect mine."

"Is that a question?" I ask after a moment, crossing my arms across my chest.

"You do that to protect us," he says without looking away from me.

His gaze is disarming.

There's an intensity there that I haven't seen before.

He was always so casual and easy-going, but I had no idea that he had this other side to him.

"You got mad at us for going out to the diner and you got upset when I went out to

The Perfect Cover

the bar. I know that you acted that way because you care. You don't want us to get caught. Well, I'm doing this for you, too."

He flips the top and lights the corner of the pages in his hands.

"I can't have this confession out here. If we get caught, they'll probably kill us. Shoot us point blank. With you, they'll have questions. They won't want to believe that you have been held captive this whole time. You'll need to prove it to them that you were. Things like this, *mistakes* like these," Mac says, holding up the burning papers to my face, "they're going to put you away for life."

I watch the pages burn knowing that he's right.

Besides, why does it matter? I have written the words down. The venom has been expelled out of me.

The mere act of writing the truth made everything better.

We walk back to the motel and just when I step on the first stair, Mac whispers, "So, who do you owe the debt to?"

My heart sinks.

It drops into the lower part of my stomach and then even further down my body.

My blood runs cold and I glance over at him.

He had skimmed the pages, but I had no idea that he had read *that* page.

I had only written about the debt a little bit, briefly touching on it, but it must've been enough.

"It's your mother's debt, right?" he asks. "You said that she had disappeared."

I shake my head and say, "I don't want to talk about it."

"I don't want to talk about a lot of things," Mac says, "but it doesn't change the fact that they get talked about when necessary."

"That's my problem. It doesn't concern you."

"No, I beg to differ. We're running for our lives. Our faces are plastered all over primetime. Everyone is looking for us. If you owe a debt to someone, we need to know about it. At least I do."

I shake my head and mock, "I bet you wish you hadn't burned all those pages now, don't you?"

17

TYLER

WHEN WE FIGHT...

Mac says that he's going out for a smoke, but he doesn't stay on the landing or out front. Instead, he disappears somewhere out back, following a trail.

I want to follow him, but I don't want to pry. Besides, the beers are hitting me pretty well and I'm not sure any comments that I'm going to make will do anyone any good.

I take a few deep breaths, lean back against the limpest pillow I've ever had, and stare at the television as I flip through the channels.

I don't know how much time passes or why

they both come in through the door at the same time.

I'm drunk but not enough to not sense the tension between them.

Mac covers it with a joke and Isabelle jumps in front of her computer screen. The fact that we're staying in less than 100 square feet is not making this trip any easier.

"Listen, I'm going to head out," Mac says, grabbing his wallet.

It's filled with money that he borrowed from me and a $100 bill that the girl he met last night had given him.

If I didn't know him, I'd suspect that the money was stolen, but I know how charming and sweet he can be and how women will fall over backward to help him.

I glance over at Isabelle, expecting her to try to stop him.

She doesn't.

I don't either.

It's not worth the energy when the outcome will be the same.

Besides, I want some alone time with her.

A few moments later, Mac exits without

another word and Isabelle and I remain, listening to the silence that he leaves behind.

"What happened?" I ask.

She buries her head behind her laptop, pretending not to hear me.

I ask her again, and again she ignores me.

"Did you have a fight? Did he do something?" I ask.

"Yeah, he did something."

I clench my fists.

He hurt her.

He could have any woman he wants except her. She said no and he pushed himself on her.

"He burned my journal," she says with tears in her eyes.

My hand opens up as I try to process what she just said.

"So, he didn't attack you?"

She stares at me, shaking her head and saying, "Yes, he did. He grabbed my journal, ripped the pages out of it, and then burned them."

"Okay, I understand. I just got scared that maybe he put his hands on you."

"Typical," she says sarcastically. "You

don't give a shit about what he actually did because you assume that at least he didn't do something way worse."

"That's not what I said," I protest.

I hate this anger that transpires between us. I don't know where it's coming from, but Mac's presence seems to be bringing out the worst in us.

I ask her about the journal and she relays the details.

I try not to be relieved by what Mac did, but I am.

I offer her sympathy but she doesn't accept it. I'm not a very good liar. If the Pittsburgh Police Department knew that, then none of this would've ever happened.

"Do you think that he did the right thing?" she says more as a statement rather than a question. Or perhaps, it's an accusation?

I shrug my shoulders. I don't want to lie to her, but I also don't want to have another fight. We don't have too much time together and that time needs to be special.

Honeymoon sort of special.

After all, I am trying to figure out if she will be the one person to know my whereabouts after I disappear for good or if she will be like the rest of them; clueless about the man I'm about to become.

"I was just writing down my thoughts. It was cathartic," Isabelle says after a long pause. "My therapist said it would help and it did. I have no intentions of keeping that journal or showing it to anyone."

"What if—" I start to say, but she cuts me off.

"I know. What if the cops stop us? What if the FBI finds it? Then they'll know that I'm not really your hostage. Mac has already given me a long lecture about this. Right before he burned the pages."

"He shouldn't have done it like that but I'm glad he did it."

"I know."

"He didn't want those pages to exist one moment longer than they had to. It's proof that your reasons for being here are false. He was just trying to protect you."

"I know," she repeats herself.

I nod, unsure as to what else to say.

"I doubt that he did it for that reason though," Isabelle says. "He's out at a bar somewhere picking up a girl. She's going to gaze into his eyes, stare at his face, while they do God knows what. She's going to remember what he looks like. She may not recognize him now, but if she ever sees his face on the news anytime in the future, she'll remember."

"I know," I say quietly.

"That's why I'm so pissed. He thinks that it's okay for him to take all of these risks but God forbid I write down one honest truth in my journal and he goes ape shit."

I'm getting tired of this conversation. As much as I enjoy Mac's company, he has been a wedge in our relationship.

Isabelle is right.

His presence is only adding risk to our travels.

We would probably be a lot further along without him, but that doesn't change the fact that I owe him.

"I can't just leave him," I say.

"I'm not saying leave him."

"Well, I can't control him either. What do you want me to do?"

She throws her hands up in the air as a sign of surrender.

The Perfect Cover

Isabelle stays up late tonight. I climb under the covers and turn off the lights.

I want to touch her, but she stays by the dining room table, typing away on her computer.

I hope she's not writing her confession, but I decide to just give her space.

Finally, she comes to bed.

"Hi," she whispers.

Her voice is soft and quiet.

There's a calmness in it now.

Perhaps even a longing.

I turn around and put my arm around her shoulder.

That's when I notice that she's not wearing a shirt. I run my hand all the way up to her neck, feeling the bareness of her skin with the back of my hand.

It's cool and soft.

As I reach down slowly, my fingers find her breasts and I give them a little squeeze.

A moment later, our lips touch. Her mouth opens and our tongues intertwine.

This time is different than the way it was before.

I'm not angry at her and she's not mad at me.

We don't need to take our frustrations out on our bodies. Instead, we just lose ourselves in each other.

She's the most beautiful woman I've ever seen. The models gracing the covers of Vogue have nothing on her and never will.

She is perfection and I feel it in my soul.

Our kiss is slow and passionate.

It's the kind that overwhelms all of your senses and yet makes you feel like you are home because you belong.

My mouth travels softly down her neck toward her collarbone. Her lips are so soft that I can feel her breath as she exhales.

I can see the moonlight peeking through the blinds, turning the whole room a shade of light blue.

I peel off her clothes slowly, meticulously.

My hands travel up and down her body feeling each curve.

Whenever she tries to reach over and touch me, I stop her.

"This is going to be all about you," I whisper as I open her legs.

The Perfect Cover

I take my time kissing her on her inner thighs first and then slowly make my way closer and closer to her core.

I feel her body wanting me.

Her whole body throbbing for mine.

She reaches over to try to pull me inside, but again I stop her.

I pull away and lay her down on her stomach, letting her settle in for whatever is about to come.

My tongue makes its way from her inner thigh and up to her nonexistent panty line.

I'm teasing her and she knows that.

Finally, I lick her and then push my fingers inside of her. She arches her back and grabs onto the sheets with both hands.

With each movement, I feel her body relax. I play her like a violin.

Whenever I feel her getting closer, I slow down and pull away.

"You're teasing me," she says.

"Of course."

"I'm going to lose it at any moment now," she says, probably only half joking.

"I want to make tonight all about you."

"What if I don't want it to be about me?"

she asks, laughing, while I go deep inside of her again.

She stares at the ceiling with her eyes open wide.

"Okay. Are you ready?" I ask.

She shakes her head no, and then nods yes. I wink at her.

Burying my head between her thighs, I send her body into convulsions. She shakes from the inside out.

The tremors run through every vein and artery within her, originating at her core and spreading out.

Her fingers and toes tense up and she arches her back higher. She tries to take a breath, but no air comes in.

One wave follows another and another, as I continue to reach further and further inside of her. My mouth is soft and my fingers are hard as I fill up every part of her.

She whispers my name as loud as she can while being unable to take a breath. After I'm done with her, I lie next to her, licking my fingers.

"I love you, Isabelle. I love the taste of you

The Perfect Cover

and I love every part of you. Don't you ever forget that."

IN THE MORNING, just as the dew forms on the railing outside, when the sun starts to illuminate the earth but doesn't quite reach the horizon, I step outside to go for a run.

All of that time inside a cell and then all of that time in the car makes me feel like my muscles are atrophying.

Of course, going on a run is the liberal interpretation of what I'm going to actually do. In truth, it wouldn't even be called a jog, or a very slow walk, but the exercise is going to be quite a change for me.

That's what I want.

The stairs are particularly difficult because of the pressure they put on my foot, but I manage to get down and then force myself to put one foot in front of the other in some sort of repetitive motion.

I barely get to the edge of the building before I realize that I have been too ambitious about my prospects, but I insist on at least going around the building. The cool desert air feels nice against my skin and it's pleasant to be outside without worrying about someone recognizing me.

When I get back to the landing leading up to our room, I see Mac outside smoking.

"You're back," I say, smiling.

"I got back a few hours ago," he says. "Maggie and I got a room a few doors down."

"Did you have a good time?" I ask, trying not to appear disapproving.

I'm supposed to be his friend, not his parent, and yet he's endangering both of us with his recklessness.

"Listen, you don't have to worry about her. She's great."

"Really?" I ask, completely unconvinced.

"Yeah, but you should be worried about Isabelle."

"Listen, she told me what you did. It was really shitty."

"Did she also tell you that she owes a debt to someone and that's why she's running away? Actually, rather her mom owes this debt, but now they're after Isabelle. The mother is already missing as is."

"Her mom? Wait, what are you talking about?"

"This is exactly what I'm talking about. You don't know the first thing about that girl.

"She's keeping secrets from you. She's not here because she's your long-lost love. She's running away. Also, whoever's after her is scaring her more than the fucking FBI. That scares the shit out of me."

My mind starts to scramble as I try to process everything that he has just said to me. I knew about the debt, somewhat, but not about a missing mother or about an inherited debt.

"You need to watch your back," Mac continues before I get a chance to respond.

"I'll meet you by the car at seven," he says, putting out a cigarette and tossing it in the trash.

I watch him disappear into his room, wondering what kind of secrets Isabelle is harboring and what they're going to cost me to find out.

18

ISABELLE

A SURPRISE...

The following morning, I wake up surrounded by a glow of happiness. I open my eyes and see Tyler, with his arms wrapped around me.

He's already dressed, so he must've gotten up, maybe even gone outside, but he climbed back into bed, and now it is me who is awake first.

The sun has already risen.

I don't want to know what time it is because then I won't be able to justify staying here in his arms.

I watch him sleep.

He takes short shallow breaths and his eyebrows move slightly, along with his eyes.

He's somewhere deep in his sleep, lost in another world, and I am here watching him from this one.

I feel like an intruder, an interloper, but I can't stop. These precious moments don't last long but, for now, they are enough.

I glance over at the other bed. It is untouched. Mac hasn't slept in it all night.

A light knock on the door startles me.

Before I can ask who it is, the knob turns and Mac walks in.

"It's after seven," he announces and I nudge Tyler who mumbles something in his sleep.

I expect Mac to be hungover and tired, but he's neither of these things. In fact, there's an alertness to him that I haven't seen since the first day that I met him.

It takes me a few nudges to wake Tyler up for good and then another fifteen minutes to get ready and leave the room.

I need some coffee and what I'm really craving is Starbucks drive-thru. Unfortunately, there isn't a Starbucks in sight.

We already got gas but I hope that the

The Perfect Cover

guys are willing to stop by and get some coffee at the next gas station.

When I come downstairs, carrying my purse and a plastic bag of all the snacks and other knickknacks that somehow didn't make it into the suitcase, I see *her*.

She is standing next to my car, kissing Mac.

"Shit," I say to myself.

Her hair is a beautiful mocha color, lustrous and full of volume. Her dress sways in the wind even though this is hardly dress weather.

She's wearing a light jacket over the top and leggings underneath. Her feet are adorned with black combat boots that remind me of the ones that were popular in the 90s.

I glance over at Tyler who looks just as dumbfounded and surprised as I do.

"What do we do?" I whisper under my breath as we continue to take steps closer and closer to them.

"I'm not sure," he says.

"Hey, guys." Mac waves. "This is Maggie. She's coming with us."

I blink once, then a second time and a third.

No, he can't be serious.

Again, I look over at Tyler who looks as surprised as I feel. He extends his hand, nevertheless.

"I know that this is super last minute, but Mac invited me and, actually, he insisted," Maggie rattles off in her bubbly sort of way.

There's an easy-going feeling to her that reminds me of Mac. I can see why the two of them got together.

It's almost as if neither of them have a worry in the world.

"I don't think this is a great idea," Tyler says after a long pause.

I'm relieved that he's the one to say it and not me.

It's on the tip of my tongue, but I don't want to be the one who is always saying no.

The smile immediately vanishes off of Maggie's face.

"Yes, of course, I totally understand," she says, throwing her hands up.

Mac narrows his eyes and pulls Tyler sternly to the side. As Maggie and I wait, I give her a slight smile and nod but don't introduce myself.

My hope is that Tyler can talk some sense into him and we can get on our way. My other hope is that she doesn't recognize their faces as the most wanted men in America.

"Okay, Maggie, why don't you get in the back with me?" Mac says, opening the door.

My mouth drops open as I glare at Tyler.

He shrugs his shoulders and rolls his eyes.

"What's going on?" I ask while we are both outside the car, after Mac climbs in the back with Maggie.

"I'll tell you about it later," Tyler says.

I get into the car disenchanted. Instead of getting rid of Mac, we now have another traveler with us.

I don't know her and she knows less than nothing about me. I don't know how much she knows about Mac and Tyler, but she's bound to find out.

Then what?

Mac and Maggie laugh and giggle in the back seat. She sounds fun, outgoing, and bouncy.

I try to give them some privacy, but it's a

small car and as the hours get long, I continue to listen in.

At first, Maggie doesn't go too much into it, just mentioning that she had some issues with her boyfriend and he left her in Oklahoma.

I overhear this fact when she relays it to Mac while they talk about something else. I want to ask what happened, yet I also don't want to get too friendly however, after spending hours in the car together, it starts to feel almost rude not being more welcoming.

Besides, I'm curious.

I ask her about herself. She tells me that she grew up in Nebraska and left home when she was twenty-two. She graduated from the University of Nebraska, left her dorm, and never went back.

She mentions that she does not have any relationship with her parents but when I ask her more about that, she just waves her hand and says that she'll need some drinks in her before she can talk about it.

"I know what you mean," I say, giving her a knowing nod. "Maybe we can talk some more tonight," I propose.

She says that she would love that.

Afterward, Tyler and I exchange looks.

He tilts his head a little bit, as if to ask why I'm being so friendly.

I shrug my shoulders and give him a little smile.

I figure that I might as well know something about her if we're going be spending all this time together.

We stop for gas a few hours later around two in the afternoon and get some lunch as well. Afterward, Maggie and I sit together in the back and the boys take the front.

"So, why are you going to California?" I ask.

"Isn't that where everyone goes when you want to run away and start a new life?"

"Yeah, I guess. Some people go to Hawaii." I laugh.

"Hey, there's an idea!"

I ask her again about why she's going to California, but again she makes a small joke and doesn't delve into it.

I appreciate the honesty.

Actually, it comes as somewhat of a relief to me because now I feel like I don't have to tell her too much about who I am and she won't take it personally.

Instead of talking about us, our conversations tend to be something a lot more meaningful and relaxing.

She asks me about my hair and skin products and I ask her about how she keeps her curls so pristine despite being on the road.

Some people would say that what we talk about is shallow, but it kind of connects us in a way. She finds out a little bit about who I am. I find out a little bit about who she is. We don't disclose anything we don't want to and yet we each get a glimpse of who we are.

I can't remember the last time I talked about clothes and makeup, music and movies with a girl before. The women I worked with, work with currently, I have to remember that I'm only here on vacation, I never talked to them much about things like that.

I probably should have.

I probably could have.

For some reason, I couldn't relax with them the same way I can with Maggie.

I wonder if it has something to do with the

fact that I don't expect to see her for a long time.

She's kind of like my single-serving friend.

There's something relaxing about being with someone like that because there isn't this pressure that you're going to see them day in and day out.

Plus, what happens if you find out something about them that you don't like?

With Maggie, I am actually surprised that we have so much in common.

"Are you okay?" Maggie asks when I get a little bit quiet and look out at the desert flickering by me.

"Yeah, I just spaced out a little bit."

"That happens to me, too, sometimes," she says in that fun bouncy way and I find it hard to believe.

"So, tell me about this ex that you mentioned," she says. "You guys went to Hawaii together?"

I can't remember exactly when I brought him up and I'm taken aback by the fact that she remembers.

"Actually, he surprised me with a trip to Hawaii. He bought the tickets and booked the resort and everything, but I kind of freaked out and couldn't go."

"Oh, no, what happened?"

I haven't talked about this much at all except with India, but somehow the words just come tumbling out.

"I had a panic attack. That morning, when we were supposed to go to the airport, I just couldn't do it. I could barely convince myself to pack a suitcase. If I had managed to get on the plane and get there, I probably would've discovered that I didn't bring anything that I needed."

"I'm really sorry," she says, placing her hand on my arm.

I shake my head and give a little shrug.

"I thought that he would understand. That was probably the hardest thing to deal with."

"He didn't?"

I shake my head and she waits for me to explain.

I look ahead and see Tyler's ears perk up, also listening. I can't remember if I ever told him the story.

"He got really mad," I say. "Angry, pissed

off, whatever you want to call it. He broke some furniture, nearly broke my face."

She gasps and then suddenly I see a different expression on her face.

It's almost as if she is someone who knows what that's like; to be with someone like that.

I can talk about it nonchalantly now even though I'm not really talking about it, I'm making jokes and making light of it.

I'm not being honest about it either, not about how I felt that night or about how scared I was that I would never make it out of there alive.

"Anyway, it all worked out for the best. He ended up going on the trip himself and he met his future wife there."

"He did?" Maggie asks, elongating the last word as if I'm giving her the juiciest piece of gossip.

I sit back and laugh, while saying, "Well, good riddance, I guess."

"Yes, of course," she says, taking my hand into hers and raising it up high. "You don't deserve that. No woman does."

I like that she's celebrating me, that she's thinking of me as some sort of symbol of women empowerment. The only problem is that I'm not.

I put up with it for way too long.

I was scared.

I was hurt.

I wasn't sure if I could get out of it. In fact, I was lucky that he got so angry that he took off on his own and ended up meeting someone else.

I don't tell her this. I have never told this to anyone out loud, but I have often wondered exactly how his wife is doing. I hope that they have a peaceful relationship. I hope that he treats her the way that she deserves to be treated.

Given what India says about men who abuse women, it is unlikely that he has improved his behavior.

But a person can have hope, right?

"I'm really sorry that you had to go through that, but I'm glad that you're with someone so much better now."

I give her a slight nod and a forced smile.

I don't want to think about the fact that if Maggie were to be interviewed by the FBI or

The Perfect Cover

the police, they would immediately find out that I am not being held hostage in this car.

"Of course, I'm not mad about it anymore," I say as casually as possible. "We were never really right for each other. He was here and I was there and our relationship was to a large degree just a convenience. We got along just well enough to keep going until it became too hard. After we broke up, I promised myself to never be with someone out of convenience again."

19

TYLER

WHEN THE LIGHTS FLASH...

When I hear the two of them in the back seat laughing and joking around, I forget that we are actually on the run.

For a moment, I actually feel like we are just two couples, four friends, taking the trip of a lifetime across America.

I try to stay in this headspace for as long as possible but old thoughts creep in.

I don't know much about Maggie and she doesn't offer much while she rides with us. She must have told Mac some sort of story and even though I doubt that it's the truth, I hope that she has enough riding on whatever it is that she's running away from to keep our secret.

I don't know how much longer I want to travel with Mac now that Maggie is here.

I still owe him a favor, a big one, but even though I haven't taken him far, I feel like I have paid him handsomely.

Having Maggie here is a danger to both me and Isabelle. Having Mac here is bad enough, but she's a bystander, an outsider.

Once she finds out about the reward, there will be nothing stopping her from turning on us and collecting the money. While I try to formulate a solid plan, an exit strategy, I keep my friendliness level up.

I don't want to be rude or a bad host. I don't want to draw attention to anything about us.

The longer that she can keep thinking that we are just three friends out on a road trip, the better we all will be.

As we get further and further into the desert, I try to figure out exactly what it is that she knows. She knows our names and some general things about us. She doesn't share much about herself and seems to be okay with the fact that we don't either.

The only thing that comes as a surprise to me is the fact that Isabelle tells her about an abusive ex-boyfriend, one that she hadn't even told me about. I wonder if they have this in common.

Perhaps it is what they bonded over while we stopped for gas and to stretch our legs. The girls speak in hushed tones in the back while Mac turns up Metallica in the front.

I sit in the front passenger seat and stare out the window at the beautiful desert that unfolds before me. If I am lucky enough to escape and start a new life, I'm never going back east. I decide this right here, right now as the shrubs whiz below the endless fucking blue sky that goes for miles and miles in all directions.

We drive for a long time today, occasionally changing drivers. I'm back behind the wheel when I see the flashing lights.

It's hard for lights to creep up on you unless you're not really paying attention, and in this case, I'm not. In fact, I haven't even seen that it was a police car because Mac and I were so deep into our conversation about whether Guns N' Roses or Led Zeppelin is the superior band.

My heart leaps into my chest as I keep checking the rearview mirror to make sure that my eyes are not deceiving me. After a moment, I look back and that's when he puts on the sirens.

I don't have much time to make a decision. I either put the pedal to the floor and gun it or pull over and try to pretend that everything is fine.

"The car is registered and I have all the paperwork," Isabelle whispers in my ear. "I think we should try to just get by."

She's right.

Of course, she's right.

The car is registered and I have a fake license with a fake name, a gift from Mac, something that we had made back in prison. That doesn't mean that it will work though.

I glance over at him and he gives me a slight nod.

"Let's try this," he says calmly.

I pull over and wait an interminable

amount of time for the cop to check the license plate. Eventually, he gets out of the car and waddles over.

He is a big man, but the way that the belt is positioned around his waist and the slow way that he is moving, he resembles a penguin.

I wait for him as I roll down the window, silently praying out of desperation, trying to remember the words that I was taught in Sunday school all those years ago.

"License and registration," he says with a slow, tired twang.

"Did I do something wrong, officer?" I ask.

"Your plates are from Pennsylvania. You're a long way from there." He points out, looking down at my driver's license.

He pokes his head in and looks at the rest of us, carefully examining each of our faces. It is only when his eyes meet mine that his lips break out into a smile.

"Your friend here was driving over the speed limit," the officer says, talking just to Maggie and no one else.

"Oh, I'm so sorry about that. He's usually

a really good driver."

"Yeah, right," the officer mumbles under his breath.

"I'll be right back," he says, taking my fake license with him.

I'm drenched in sweat. I rub the palms of my hands on my pants trying to wipe off the perspiration, but it's all to no avail.

I start to feel so lightheaded that I feel like I'm about to pass out.

What the hell are we going to do if he knows who we are?

Unfortunately, there's only one answer to that question and I don't dare to even consider it.

I glance over at Mac and he gives me a wink.

I don't know what he means.

I shrug.

"You know what," he says under his breath.

My chest tightens.

Unlike Mac, I have never taken anyone's life.

I never wanted to.

I have talked a big game with Isabelle

about what I might have to do to gain my freedom, but if I were to hurt this cop, then whatever chance I have of proving my innocence will go out the window.

If a cop gets killed, then it doesn't really matter if I really killed my wife and her lover because I will have *his* blood on my hands.

Time slows down and each second feels like an hour.

I wait.

I look in the rearview mirror and watch him run my information through his channels.

I watch for any indication that something might be wrong, but he betrays nothing.

A few long minutes later, the cop finally climbs out of his vehicle and begins his long walk toward me.

20

TYLER

WHEN HE COMES BACK...

With the window down, I smell the dryness in the air. My skin is parched and squeaky clean.

It's a strange sensation.

My mouth is dry, yes, but the rest of me feels almost slick with cleanliness.

Watching the police officer approach the car and the way that his hat covers his eyes as he walks, I realize that I should probably tell Isabelle that I love her.

I haven't said it to her yet. Honestly, until this very moment, I wasn't sure if I did. But suddenly, it's all so clear.

I open my mouth and hold the words on the tip of my tongue.

Then I hesitate.

Mac is getting ready for battle. He doesn't have a weapon, as far as I know, but he has powerful fists and an even more powerful imagination.

Back in prison, he was able to make anything into a weapon, even the most innocuous objects. If I were to turn around and tell Isabelle that I love her, he might take that as a sign.

No, he *would* take it as a sign.

But that's not the kind of signal I want to send. I want him to stand down. I want to deescalate this situation.

Mac is ready to fight and I'm not. Not if it means endangering Isabelle's life.

The cop walks up slowly and I brace myself by holding on tightly to the steering wheel.

My jaw flexes and I force it to relax.

"Here you go," he says, handing me the driver's license and registration through the open window. "I'm going to let you off with a warning for now, but make sure you don't go over the speed limit again. They are there for a reason."

The Perfect Cover

I don't let out a sigh of relief until he gets back into his vehicle.

"Okay," Mac says. "Let's go, let's get the fuck out of here."

Maggie starts to talk again, but the three of us sit there in silence, stunned by what has just happened.

Did we really just get away? I ask myself. It's all over now.

Before I can fully come to terms with it, he comes back.

Only this time, he doesn't just trail behind me. The lights flash right from the get-go.

My heart jumps into my throat.

The cop knows exactly who we are and he wants to arrest us.

"Is that him again?" Isabelle asks.

I keep driving, unsure as to what to do.

"Maybe he forgot something?" Maggie asks. "Maybe we should stop?"

Maybe, but that's not what's going to happen. I press the pedal all the way to the floor and gun it.

"What are you doing?"

Everyone knows what I'm doing. I'm trying to get away with our lives.

The police car follows behind.

When I hit eighty miles per hour, so does he.

When I get up to ninety and then ninety-five, he does as well.

Eventually, we start racing down the dark desert at over one hundred ten miles per hour, swishing around cars.

I don't have much time for a plan. He has already called for backup and that means at any on-ramp there could be ten new cops waiting for us.

When I see an exit coming up, I create as much of a separation between us as I can and pray that there are no other cars getting off.

Then I flick off my headlights and drive up the exit. The bend in the road gives me a little bit of time. I pray that it is enough for me to lose him.

As soon as I get on the overpass, I turn on the lights and slow down to a normal speed, to match the other drivers'. We hold our breaths.

There's a loud and busy truck stop at the far end and I pull into the parking lot to hide in the shadows. I kill the engine and the lights and wait.

Doubt starts to creep in.

Should I have kept going?

Is sitting here and waiting the best thing to do?

A few minutes pass and then five more. After twenty minutes, I start to feel like maybe we're safe. At least for now.

"What's going on?" Maggie keeps asking. "Why are y'all running away from cops?"

No one answers for a while.

Then Isabelle says, "You don't want to know."

"Ready to go back?" I ask Mac and Mac only.

He gives me a slight nod.

"Any chance that he's waiting for us there?"

"There's always a chance, but I'm not sure. I think he would've followed us on here if he knew that's where we went."

I swallow hard and drive as normal as possible. There's no flashing lights anywhere, but that doesn't mean he's not waiting with other unmarked vehicles.

Still, the only thing I can do is drive and that's exactly what I do.

I don't feel safe stopping so I keep driving. Instead of staying on the interstate, I get off and drive north. No one argues with me.

After a few hours, everyone falls asleep, but my adrenaline keeps pumping and I keep driving.

I want to get us as far away as possible and never get that close to danger again.

Around three in the morning, I pull into an empty, almost abandoned gas station and am pleasantly surprised that the pump actually works. Maggie and Mac are asleep, but Isabelle comes out to get some fresh air with me.

"That was really scary," she says, rubbing her shoulders to warm up.

"Yeah, it was."

"We need a new car," she says quietly.

"Yes, I know. I've been trying to figure out how to do that for the last two hours."

"She can't keep traveling with us," Isabelle says. "She's on the verge of finding out who you are if she doesn't already know. And if we run into the cops again, they're going to shoot to kill—"

The Perfect Cover

I cut her off by putting my finger up to her mouth.

"I agree," I say quietly. I know everything that she's thinking and I don't want to talk about it. "Kiss me."

I pull her close to me and hold her for a long time. I can feel her body soften against mine. When she looks up at me, I press my lips onto hers.

21

ISABELLE

WHEN WE STOP...

When we get to the motel, I tell Tyler that I want to get two rooms and no one fights me on it.

When we get to ours, I practically run inside, toss my bag onto the bed, and yell, "What the fuck was that?"

Dumbfounded rather than overly excited like I am, Tyler plops down on the other queen bed and stares at the ceiling.

Neither of us can believe that we actually got away with it. The cop should have caught up with us. He should have caught us.

"We were incredibly lucky," I say. "I don't think that's going to happen again."

Tyler nods and continues to stare straight ahead. I pace around the motel room trying to figure out what to do.

"If Maggie didn't suspect anything about us earlier, she undoubtably will now. She's spending the night with Mac and who knows what he's going to tell her."

"You're not telling me anything that I don't already know," Tyler says.

There is a monotone quality to his voice.

It's almost as if he is absent from the conversation. It's as if he's not really here.

I don't know where to begin.

I don't know what decisions we have to make first, but I do know that we need to get a new car.

I want to grab Tyler and shake him out of his coma, but I restrain myself.

I feel like I am becoming more and more hysterical. Somehow pacing around and getting my body moving is making everything worse.

I hold the phone in my palm and actually consider calling India for help. She has always been a sound voice in my head, especially when I did not have one of my own.

The Perfect Cover

"Tyler," I say, sitting down on the edge of the bed.

I nag him to move his feet out of the way and to make room, but he only does it after I kick him again.

"The cops are after us," I say quietly. "When that cop went after us the second time, he found out something about us. I don't know what exactly, but I doubt that it was anything good."

"I know," Tyler agrees. "What do you want me to do about it?"

"We need a plan. If he knows who you are…" My voice trails off.

I don't exactly know how to continue. The truth is that if he knows who Tyler is, then all the cops in the state are probably looking for us.

Our car is parked right out front and perhaps that's the stupidest thing we have done so far.

"If the cops know the make, model, and the license plate of my car," I say, "then it's not going to be very difficult for them to find us."

"Do you want to leave?" Tyler asks.

I shrug my shoulders.

I do, but I don't.

I want to get some rest.

I feel like I need it, but I also don't know if we're making a terrible mistake. I really hope not.

"I know that Mac is your closest friend," I say after a long pause. I need to approach this topic very carefully, treading lightly. "I know that he saved you and that you owe him, but I don't think it's a good idea to travel with Mac and Maggie anymore."

"I don't either," Tyler says, surprising me.

"You don't?"

"Of course not. Especially not Maggie. She's an outsider. He just met her. If she finds out the truth about us, then it's all over."

"So, what should we do?"

"I have no idea," he says. "All I know is that we can't just leave them."

I stare into his big beautiful eyes and then somewhere past him. The headboard is made of some sort of strange combination of Formica and oak.

It's scuffed up from years of use. I focus my eyes on one particular gouge. It runs perpendicular from one side to the other as if someone had taken a nail to it and scratched it up on purpose.

Tyler is right. We can't just leave them.

Not only is it a really shitty thing to do, but it would also be dangerous for us. They would have no money and they would have no options.

What if Mac turned on us and told the authorities where we are in exchange for a better deal?

What about Maggie?

She would undoubtably take that reward money and help the FBI. She owes us no allegiance.

As I go through all of these scenarios in my mind, coming up empty with any possibility, Tyler sits up and puts his hand on my knee.

He gives it a little squeeze. It's reassuring at first, comforting even.

I force a little smile in commiseration. Just as the world starts to feel like it's closing in on me, he leans over and kisses me.

It takes me by surprise and a wave of relief washes over me.

"No, I can't," I say, pulling away from him.

"What do we have to lose?" he asks, trying to kiss me again.

"It's not that. I'm just not in the mood. I feel like the world is on fire and there's nothing I can do to put out all the fires."

"It's not on fire *yet*. I have seen it on fire and this is just smoke."

"It's coming from somewhere and it's closing in on us. If we don't make the right decisions… It's all going to disappear."

"If that's the case," Tyler whispers, pulling me closer to him, "then why don't you just close your eyes and let me take you to another planet?"

He wanders his fingers down my neck and over my breasts, but suddenly, his touch just makes me recoil.

"It's like you're not listening to me," I say, standing up. "This doesn't feel right. I can't do this until we figure out what is going on."

"We won't know what's going on until the cops find us and arrest us."

"You're saying it like it's a certainty."

"Is it not?" he asks, his eyes glaring at mine.

"I don't know what you're talking about. If you're going to have this defeatist attitude, then I can't deal with it," I say sternly.

"Is it defeatist or am I just accepting the truth?" he asks.

He has talked like this before and I've always hated it.

"What are we even doing here? I mean, why are we even running away? I thought that you were after something. I thought that you wanted to prove your innocence."

He looks down at the floor.

I can tell that he's devastated.

I can also tell that he didn't really mean what he said.

"I know that this whole thing has been really difficult," I start to say, "but we have to start making decisions that are best for us. Maggie is not part of that equation. Mac used to be, but not anymore. It's just too dangerous."

"I know," Tyler says. "I wonder if it's more dangerous to leave them."

We talk about this for a while. Long after we should have already gone to sleep.

It's not that difficult to drive, but the days

are long and now we are way off course for getting to California.

We are much more north than we should have been and I have no idea how much farther north we should go.

There are so many unknowns and yet none of these questions seem to be possible to answer tonight.

Tyler tries to kiss me again. I love the way that he makes me feel and I love losing myself in his body. But tonight, it doesn't feel right.

I'm just too overwhelmed, exhausted, and overtired.

"It's going to make you feel better," he insists, playing with my hair and kissing the back of my neck.

"I can't," I say. "I'm going to take a shower."

I get up and head to the bathroom.

"Can I join you?" he asks.

"No, I need some alone time," I say and close the door behind me.

After a very long and hot shower, so hot in fact that my face becomes beet red and stays that way for a while, I come back into the main room and see Tyler fast asleep.

The Perfect Cover

Still dressed in his clothes, he's curled up in the fetal position, facing the window. I take a blanket and wrap it around him and turn off the lights.

It takes me a while to fall asleep. When I finally do, it seems like I have to be up again.

My alarm goes off at 6:30 a.m. but I press the snooze button three times before I can finally pull myself out of bed.

After going to the bathroom and brushing my teeth, I come out and see Tyler sitting on the edge of the bed staring at the television, which is turned to the local news channel and placed on mute.

"What's wrong?" My heart sinks. "Did they say something about us?" I ask, walking quickly toward him.

He shakes his head and hands me a piece of paper. It's a small note, written on a page from the Bible in the nightstand.

We had to go.

It's too dangerous to travel together.
See you later or in another life.
Thanks for everything, Mac.

. . .

I READ the words over and over again. They're written in large letters and red ink.

"He's gone?" I ask.

I run over to the window. A wave of relief washes over me when I see that the car is still parked out front.

"They're gone," Tyler says. "So is the money."

22

TYLER

WHEN WE LEAVE...

After we discover that Mac and Maggie have taken off with all of our money, leaving us with only the $200 that Isabelle had stashed away in her purse, we don't stick around long.

We head straight out onto the road. Isabelle keeps trying to talk to me, but I just need a few minutes, more like a few hours, to figure out how it all went so wrong.

They left us the car, but the car is compromised. I have to assume that there's an All-Points Bulletin put out on it and every cop in the state is looking for us.

We would be incredibly lucky if this were

not the case, but that's the assumption that we have to make.

"I just don't understand. How could he have gotten the money?" Isabelle keeps asking.

She's racking her brain, trying to figure out exactly when he got into her purse or how he even knew that she had kept the money in different envelopes around her bag.

"Mac is a thief," I finally admit. "That's not why he was in prison, but that was how he had made his living for a long time. He was a professional thief."

"What are you talking about?"

"I don't know how else to say it."

"Like he would break into liquor stores and rob them?"

I shake my head and say, "Like he would break into banks, steal thousands of dollars, and get away with it. Like he would steal paintings that are worth half a million dollars. Like he would get expensive jewels from high-end jewelry stores. He was an expert in that sort of thing. He told me all about it. For a long time, he worked with different guys. One of the best was this guy named Nicholas Crawford. They did the biggest jobs together out in New England, mostly around Cape Cod and the Hamptons, where all the rich people have their second homes. He's the one who taught him everything that he knew."

"Why did he have to steal from me?" she asks in that innocent, wide-eyed sort of way that breaks my fucking heart.

"He needed the money and that's what he does. Mac doesn't have allegiance to anyone but himself. Maybe that makes him cruel or egotistical, but that's also what makes him a survivor. I didn't realize that he knew that you had the money. Did you tell Maggie?"

She shakes her head vigorously from side to side.

"Then he must have searched your stuff when we weren't looking. He probably assumed that you had some money and when he made the decision to split, that's when he took it."

"How could he just take off like that? He doesn't even have a car."

"There was a truck stop right nearby. Nobody hitchhikes anymore, or so everyone says, except that truckers still pick up strangers and hitchhikers will gravitate toward truck stops to get where they need to go."

"So, you think a trucker is giving them a ride?"

"Probably. They're a nice-looking couple. Safe. Why not?"

She keeps asking me questions about Mac like it's somehow going to change what he did.

I tell her as much as I know, which isn't really that much at all. I know that he had a past, but I never thought that he would cross me like this.

At one point, Isabelle gets so frustrated that she begins to cry. I want to pull over and put my arm around her, but when I put on my blinker to get off at the exit, she stops me. She wipes her eyes and says to keep going.

I know that we need to get rid of this car, but I'm not sure about trying to hitchhike. If the cops know about the car, then they also know what she looks like.

I ask her to look up stuff on Google and read any new reports. There's no guarantee that the cops aren't keeping the information private, but at least it would give us something.

Isabelle searches her phone for a while

without saying much and I appreciate the silence. It's nice to be able to relax even when I probably shouldn't be.

I turn up the music of Nirvana's "Heart Shaped Box" and I take myself mentally out of the moment to another place where things aren't so fucked up.

"I couldn't find any articles about me in any of them," she says, turning down the volume before the song is over.

"Well, that's a relief."

"I guess," she says.

"They could be lying. They could be keeping some information private."

She gives me a nod.

"It could be the truth," she says. "We have no way of knowing if that cop knew anything about who we really are. We have no idea why he was going to pull us over again."

"It was probably nothing good." I point out.

"Yeah, that's true, but it doesn't have to be about the truth. Who the hell knows? You might've had a broken taillight. Maybe he had another question. From what I've read and I've read a lot of stuff, there's no mention of me and there's no mention of this car."

"That's good," I say, trying to be more positive about the situation.

"Maybe we should take it at face value," Isabelle suggests. "We have no evidence that this is not true. If we overreact and get rid of the car, if we try to hitchhike, that's just more of an opportunity for the cops to catch us."

I agree with her and also say, "I think that it might be a good idea for you to change your appearance."

It takes me a bit to convince her, but eventually she agrees.

Maggie and Mac know what she looks like and if they are caught, then they will give a certain description to the cops.

If her look doesn't fit that description, then there's a good chance that a random passerby won't be able to identify her.

23

ISABELLE

WHEN I CHANGE...

Tyler keeps urging me to color my hair and to chop it off, but the fact that I have to do this just makes me angry.

I know that he's right. I know that it's probably the safe thing to do, but every decision that I have been making is bringing me closer and closer to going to prison.

"How did I get here?" I ask myself as I wander through the aisles of the Rite Aid somewhere in Nevada.

I don't want to color my hair and I don't want to cut it. It doesn't seem like a big deal, perhaps it wouldn't be for anyone else, but for some reason it's almost devastating to me. It seems like this is the outward manifestation of every bad decision that I have made ever since I met him.

I look at the hair colors and go with a light blonde color. It reminds me of the Sun-In I used to put in my hair in high school. The dirty blonde, a few shades lighter than my natural mousy brown, is a better match for my skin color than the darker color that Tyler wants.

Along with the box, I also pick up a baseball hat, scissors, and some additional makeup. Mac and Maggie have only seen me in my travel, without makeup look. Something tells me that if I dress myself up a little bit, I will be a lot harder to recognize.

I walk past the aisle of lipsticks and debate whether I should go with a bright red. I buy it and another shade of light blush, a more neutral tone.

We only have $200 and I know that this is a major splurge, but I don't give a fuck. Tyler owes me big time for everything that I have gone through and I expect him to pay me back. He keeps promising me that he will.

That silent partner of his is supposed to

make all of our problems go away, but something in the back of my head makes me think that maybe things aren't going to be that rosy once we get to California either.

Tyler wants to drive through the night and I'm fine with that as long as I can take a nap in the back seat. We stop briefly at a truck stop so that we can get some dinner and I can color my hair.

It takes about half an hour to process so I sit in the shower room and scroll through the news on my phone. I keep checking to see whether they have linked my name or face but find nothing.

So far, I'm good. If the cops are suspecting my involvement, then they are not saying so publicly.

My new hair turns out even nicer than I thought it would. It brings out the green in my eyes and actually makes me look quite pretty.

"You look awesome," Tyler says back in the car. "Do you want to pull over on a dark road and let me do some bad things to you?"

I laugh.

"Do you think I'm kidding?" he asks. "I'm not."

"Do you like it short?" I ask, pointing to the new hairline that falls right above my shoulders.

"It's probably not short enough, but yes, it looks really good."

"Not short enough?" I gasp. "What are you talking about? That's like two inches!"

"Exactly. I was thinking of something close to your ears."

"No, no, no," I say and shake my head.

"Okay, fine, I'm not going to make you. I just want to protect you."

"Yeah, I know," I say.

Tyler reaches over and places his hand on my knee. I put my hand on top of his and squeeze tightly.

Holding his hand in mine makes me feel very safe. I know that's probably a stupid thing to think, despite everything that has happened, but I like how he makes me feel.

Before I met Tyler, my life was fraught with anxieties. Somehow, they have all been supplanted by real fears, but still, with him by my side, I feel safe. Safer than I have in a long time.

"I'm kind of glad that Mac isn't here

The Perfect Cover

anymore," I say after a long pause. "Maggie, too. It's nice just being here with you."

"I know what you mean," he says, giving me a smile as we drive further and further into the dark desert.

24

TYLER

WHEN WE GET THERE...

It's early morning when we finally pull into Palm Desert, California. It's so early in fact that I feel like we have to waste some time before we can actually stop by for a visit. It has to be at least after six.

Tessa lives in a very unassuming development at the end of a cul-de-sac. Actually, it seems like the whole city is one development after another. Some are gated, most are sprawling and expansive.

The ones with golf courses have guards and little booths out front with large gates that slide in and out. Some have enormous fountains to welcome visitors and residents. Most are lined with tall palm trees.

Luckily, for me, Tessa's house doesn't have a guard or a gate. It's just a cul-de-sac nestled among ten others, bordering a busy street.

The sky is blue, without a cloud for miles. The humidity is low and the sun is harsh. It's not even morning really and the sun feels stronger than it ever felt back home.

Without the cloud coverage, there isn't anything holding it back. That's what's appealing about this. Most residents are men and women in their 50s and 60s who start their days early by either jogging, cycling, or walking their pooches.

I glance over at Isabelle who is still curled up and asleep in the back. I decide that there is no reason to rouse her and instead park near a No Parking sign and wait until it becomes a more reasonable hour to accept uninvited guests.

Around seven a.m., I start to feel myself drift off under the warm California sun. My mouth is parched and I finish the last of the bottle of water I got in Nevada hours ago. I wish that I had pulled into a gas station or Starbucks for some coffee, but I was worried about being caught on camera.

The Perfect Cover

"Are we here?" Isabelle asks, sitting up and stretching out in both directions.

She moves her head from side to side and then holds her neck up as if she has a crick in it.

"Are you okay?" I ask.

"I must've slept funny."

"Honda Accords are not known for their comfortable sleeping arrangements," I joke.

She peeks out of the window and looks up at the enormous palm tree.

"We're here," she announces with a smile. "We're actually here?"

I give her a slight nod. "That's her house right over there."

"Why didn't you wake me up earlier?"

"It's still early. She is an early riser but I didn't want to bother her at six."

"Yeah. That's probably a good thing," Isabelle agrees, "since you are asking her to pay you a lot of money."

"Hey, it's my money. She owes it to me."

"I wasn't saying that it wasn't." She smiles.

After climbing into the front seat, Isabelle looks around.

"Honestly, I never thought that someone that wealthy would live here."

"You don't think this is a nice neighborhood?"

"Of course, it is. I mean, you can see that just by looking at it, but is it a very *wealthy* neighborhood? Like Kardashian wealthy? Like ten million-dollar homes wealthy? I don't know."

I agree with her. It looks like an upper middle class place with manicured lawns. There are no weeping willows or impressive oaks like we have back east, but the landscaping is well-maintained and pristine.

"How much longer do you want to wait?" Isabelle asks.

I look at my phone. It's half past.

Tessa is an early riser and she's probably getting her morning coffee. It's not the best time to visit an old friend, but I don't have the energy to wait any longer.

"Let's go," I say, getting out of the car.

"You don't want to park in front of her house?" Isabelle asks.

I shake my head no.

The Perfect Cover

I don't want any of her neighbors who all park their cars in their garages taking note of a strange car in their cul-de-sac. If it's out here on the main street, then no one is going to pay attention to it.

Tessa Henderson lives at the end of a cul-de-sac, about five houses in. There are only twelve houses all around, but with their two or three car garages, it takes a good five minutes to walk to her place.

Her front door is hidden around the corner from her garage and is surrounded by lush green hedges and purple flowers spilling over the top. There is a grandiose Pepper tree, tall and magnificent, right up front.

The front door is surrounded by windows on both sides, the kind of luxury that only people who live in safe neighborhoods allow themselves.

I look for a knocker, but it's a modern door and it doesn't have one. There is a small doorbell to the right side, hidden in the wall.

Isabelle stands a little bit behind me.

When I press the buzzer, a loud piercing sound consumes the house. I see a tiny little dog fly out from the corner and bust ass toward the front door.

Fearless and full of venom the way that little dogs tend to be, she stands on her back legs and challenges me with all of her might.

A moment later, Tessa walks up to the door. She's dressed in an embroidered bathrobe with her hair up in a turban. She reminds me of some sort of exotic widow from a fifties movie.

I have never seen her look this way. Usually, she is dressed in an unassuming and serious way.

Nothing too flashy. Nothing too opulent.

Yet here she is answering the door in a robe that you'd imagine a Vegas lounge singer would wear on her days off.

I can feel Isabelle's body tense up behind me, but as soon as Tessa opens the door and throws her arms around me, we both let out a sigh of relief.

"Tyler? Is this really you?" she asks.

Before I can answer, she pulls me inside, along with Isabelle and shuts the door quickly behind us.

"Is this really you? You look great!"

"You, too," I say, pointing to her attire.

"Well, you get bored wearing the same exact bathrobe all the time, you know?" she asks casually.

"This is my friend, Isabelle," I say, turning around.

25

ISABELLE

WHEN I MEET HER...

I can tell that Tyler was nervous coming here, but Tessa actually puts me at ease. She has a motherly type of demeanor even though I don't think she has kids.

I like her robe and her plush pink turban. I like the casual way in which she pops up her glasses and uses them to accentuate her sentences.

She doesn't seem annoyed that we're here so early and gets busy making breakfast and coffee. I keep insisting that I don't want anything, but she practically bullies me into eating her pancakes.

"It's so nice to have guests," she says.

"Especially, a longtime friend who I haven't seen in a while."

"So, you have known each other for a while?" I ask.

"Yeah, you could say that."

"A few lifetimes at least," Tyler adds.

The two of them reminisce a bit about the past. Tessa tells me about getting her PhD at the University of Pittsburgh.

"I majored in organic chemistry," she says. "I got offered a job at a lab but I wanted to continue going to school so I ended up going to grad school. After that, I worked in a lab for many years. It was rewarding. I wish that I'd tried teaching, but I didn't."

"Why not?" I ask.

"I like to keep to myself. I don't like a lot of interactions and interruptions throughout the day."

"Really?" I ask, finding that hard to believe given how nice she's being now.

"Well, it's not every day that you see a ghost," she says, leaning back against the kitchen counter and looking Tyler up and down.

The Perfect Cover

I open my mouth to ask her more about that, but Tyler beats me to it.

"It got pretty bleak in there," he says quietly. "If it weren't for the money that you sent…" His voice trails off and we all take a moment of silence.

"I'm glad that I could do anything to help you. That was really fucked up what happened."

I nod, hoping that she will elaborate.

When Tyler excuses himself to use the restroom, she does.

"I'm glad that you believe in his innocence," Tessa says.

"The thing is that the prosecution had such a tight case."

"No, they didn't. They had no case. They railroaded him."

"He didn't really have an alibi," I say.

It's not that I'm arguing for his guilt, it's just that I want her to give me more proof that she has of his innocence.

"Oh, you don't know, do you?" Tessa asks, taking a sip of her black coffee with no sugar or cream.

"Know what?"

"Tyler doesn't have an alibi because he was with me when it happened, but he kept that information from the cops because that's the kind of person that he is."

I feel all the blood drain away from my face.

"Wait, I don't understand," I mutter.

"They convicted him largely because he didn't have an alibi for where he was the night of the murder. Well, he was with me."

"Why didn't you…"

Tessa takes a step away from me and looks down at me through her reading glasses.

"Isabelle, you're not seriously asking me this question, are you?"

"Yes, I am. He got life in prison for two murders that he did not commit. He could've gotten the death penalty. He would be there now if he hadn't escaped. Yet, he had an alibi this whole time."

"You do realize what kind of business I'm in, right?" she asks, the expression on her face suddenly becoming grave and distant.

I give her a nod.

"We can't discuss the details, but I want to at least tell you that your boyfriend is a very honorable man. I asked him not to tell them where he was the night of the murders and he didn't. Not when he was arrested, not when he was on trial, not when he was convicted."

I have so much more to ask her, but Tyler returns.

"Oh, shit," Tyler says, looking at me. "You didn't tell her, did you?" he asks Tessa.

"She wanted to make sure that you didn't actually kill your wife," Tessa says, sitting down in her chair with a little smile at the corner of her lips. "She traveled all this way with you, committing who knows how many felonies, but she still wanted to double-check that everything was on the up and up."

"That's not what happened," I say sternly. "I just asked you if you happen to have any more proof about his innocence. Anything that he could use to prove that he didn't do it."

"Well, I told you what I have, whether or not you use it is up to Tyler."

Luckily, our conversation is cut short when Tessa excuses herself to take a phone call in another room. We sit in her bright kitchen overlooking a turquoise pool and hot tub.

The sun is bright and the weather is warm. The hedges out back provide what feels like infinite privacy.

"You had an alibi this whole time and you didn't say anything?" I ask Tyler, not wanting to waste a moment of our alone time.

"It's not that easy, Isabelle. This is the drug business. I can't just tell the cops that I was with her without implicating Tessa and everybody who works for her."

"What were you doing?"

He shakes his head.

"Tell me," I insist.

He thinks about it for a moment.

"It was just a meeting. She came to me because she needed some help with the drug cartel out of Mexico."

The phrase drug cartel makes my mouth drop open. My throat gets parched and I swallow hard.

"I don't know the details of her operation and I don't want to, but I was with her that night and there were other people there. They showed up. They talked in private, but I couldn't very well tell the police that I was with *her*. I had to keep my mouth shut in order to not get killed. The thing that they say about snitches on television is true. If anyone suspects that you will open your mouth about anything that happens, they take you out. They don't debate and they don't second-guess."

"I don't understand," I say, shaking my head. "Were you actually involved in the drug deal?"

"No. She was my silent partner, my investor, remember? We had a meeting about her money, she wanted to invest more. Essentially launder it. She needed to clean it in order to pay taxes and buy a house and a car and be a normal person. That's partly what the hedge fund was doing for her. When we had that meeting, I had no idea that those guys were going to show up. Luckily, nothing bad happened and I thought it would all work out. I had no idea that was the night that my wife and her lover would get killed."

Before I get a chance to ask him to elaborate more, Tessa comes back.

"So, kid, why don't you tell me the tale

about how you managed to escape from a maximum-security institution?"

While Tyler talks, I try to figure out what compelled him to not tell the authorities about his alibi. I realize that we're talking about a cartel and drugs worth millions of dollars, but there's also his life.

How could he not stand up for himself?

How could he go down for a crime that he didn't commit all in an effort to not reveal who he was with that night?

After breakfast, we go outside on the patio to have a second round of coffee while the birds are chirping.

"You know, you don't seem to be very surprised to see us," I say, taking a sip.

"Well, I was expecting to hear from Tyler after I heard about his escape."

"You were?" I ask.

"Of course. I'm sure that he told you that I am in quite a lot of debt to him and of course, I plan to pay him back every penny."

"Uh-huh," I mumble.

"I'm not avoiding talking to you about that, Tyler," Tessa says. "Let me be perfectly clear with you. I don't have the money."

The Perfect Cover

I see the expression on Tyler's face change from friendly to aloof.

"What are you talking about?" he asks, furrowing his brows.

"Is business not going well?"

"It's not that. It's actually going quite well. That's why I have very little to offer you. It's all tied up in investments. I had no idea that you would be getting out of prison. I thought that I would be paying you in small bits here and there. I can do that."

"You don't have any money?" Tyler asks again, cocking his head.

I can tell that he doesn't quite believe her or maybe he's just trying to assess the situation.

"It's hard to explain, but the gist is that no, I don't have any of it. The most I can offer you now is a couple thousand."

Tyler shakes his head and the blood drains away from his face. "That's not enough, Tessa. That's not nearly enough."

"I know," she starts to say.

"You owe me $300,000," he says. "In cash. You said that I could have it back at any time. We never had a payment plan. You're not supposed to be investing that money in anything."

"I know and I didn't. I thought you would need it for your defense or your appeal or something like that. I held onto it for a while and then an emergency came up. Listen, I don't have to explain myself to you."

"Yes, you do. You owe me 300 grand and I expect it back."

"You will have it back, just not today."

26

ISABELLE

WHEN WE LEAVE...

The motel is less than a five minute drive away from her house, but it feels like a century passes before we get there.

When we leave, I wait for him to start talking but he doesn't. When we get to the car and get onto Monterey, a large busy road that takes us down to the motel, my thoughts spin out of control.

The houses are getting nicer the more south we go. There is a huge mountain, the color of sand, rising from the ground. The sun is beating down hard, it's harsh and unfiltered through lack of clouds. The air feels crisp, hovering at just over 8% humidity. I cough lightly to clear my throat and a loose droplet lands on the back of my hand and dries almost in an instant.

"Are we not going to talk about this?" I ask Tyler when he pulls into the empty parking lot of a double-decker hotel.

There are about ten rooms and each door looks straight outside, facing the highway.

As he tries to get out of the car, I put my hand on his knee.

"She owes you a lot of money," I whisper.

"Yes, I know," he says with a sigh.

"What are we going to do? Mac left us with $200. How much do we have left? $150?"

"I know," he says.

"The whole point was to get here and to get the money." I continue.

I feel my voice getting urgent and tense. It's mirroring what's happening on the inside.

"I'm going to figure something out."

On the outside, he doesn't seem fazed by any of this. Hardly even bothered.

It's either that or I haven't gotten a good sense of his moods. Perhaps, he's just distant. Not entirely here.

"Is something wrong? Why don't you think that this is a bigger deal than it is?"

Frustrated, he gets out of the car and slams the door in my face.

I'm losing control.

My heart is beating out of my chest.

My palms get sweaty. I try to calm myself by getting out of the car, closing my eyes and pointing my face toward the sun.

I take a few deep breaths with my diaphragm and feel a little better.

I've never tried to meditate, but I wonder if this is what it's like, just standing here and shutting the world out and not letting it in, no matter what.

A few minutes later, I follow Tyler to the front desk. I'm supposed to be doing this. We're supposed to be careful, but neither of us are thinking clearly right now.

Luckily, the clerk out front has her nose buried in her phone and barely bothers to look up once.

"Usually, the normal check-in is at two, but you're in luck," she says. "We actually have a room for you."

"Thank you," I say. "We really appreciate that."

When we get to the room, it's not even ten a.m.. I know that we're lucky to get in so early, but I don't feel lucky at all.

Two more nights and we will have to start sleeping in the car. Or we'll have to take that couple of thousand dollars that Tessa offered and forget about the rest, at least for a while.

But how long will that last? And then what?

"I NEED TO TALK TO YOU," I say, turning to Tyler after we drop our bags on the floor.

"Not now," he mumbles.

"No, *yes*, now," I insist.

"What do you want me to say?" Tyler asks. "You heard everything that she said."

"You have to insist. You have to make her. She's lying."

"No. Tessa is many things, but she's not a liar. She's going to pay us back. She just doesn't have the money and that's not an excuse."

The Perfect Cover

"Well, I don't know, but we have to do something. We can't just do nothing, right?"

"Yes, we do have to do something."

I wait for him to continue, but Tyler just shuts down. He plops on the bed and turns on the TV. I hate the way that he is ignoring me but there isn't much I can do.

I start to talk again, I try to push him to say something… Meaningful, but nothing comes out.

"I just don't understand how you can let her treat you like that," I blow up.

The rage that has been boiling up within me from the time that Mac showed up and then Maggie showed up, suddenly comes spilling out.

The frustration feels like impotence. And it's difficult to describe.

"I'm not letting her do anything," Tyler says calmly. "We'll talk about this later."

"No!" I yell.

"I'm not going to talk to you while you're angry like this."

"Don't you get it? My anger isn't going to get better with time. It's not just going to disappear. It's going to get worse. I need an answer."

He says, "Stop," and flashes his eyes at me.

He narrows them and a coldness that I haven't seen before washes over them.

"This isn't up to you, Isabelle. This has nothing to do with you. This is *my* money and this is *my* problem. If you don't want to be a part of my life anymore, then you can just go home."

"Well, I'd love to!" I yell. "But the problem is that I fucking can't! I don't have any fucking money!"

My body tenses from all the anger as it courses through my veins.

I grab my purse and keys and slam the door behind me.

Maybe Tyler is right, I do need some space. At least some time away from him to figure out how the fuck to get back home.

I take the car and drive around for a while, but the stoplights and the other cars just make me feel angrier and more out of control.

Luckily, when I pull onto a small road going toward the hills, I see a sign for a trail. I turn and it leads me to a parking lot in front of a trailhead.

I grab an old bottle of water that sits in the cupholder along with the keys to the car and my phone. I tuck my crossbody bag under the passenger seat so that it's out of sight and lock the car on my way out.

The beginning of the trail is rocky but doesn't have much of an incline until I make it past a big boulder and then the road feels like I'm scaling a mountain.

The rocks beneath my feet are different shades of beige and brown. Some are small like pebbles and others are jagged and uneven, waiting to trip me.

The trail is clearly marked and used, but it's thin and narrow. About a quarter of a mile in, I glance back at the developments and the hedges below. The valley is spotted with palm tree heads, filling the horizon with spots of color.

The further away I get from the motel, the easier I breathe. My chest relaxes and the deeper I can inhale.

I try to focus my mind on the problem at

hand by not thinking about it at all. In fact, I don't even think about Tyler.

Despite the fact that I love him, there are parts of him that make my blood boil.

It's the part that shuts down when I need him most.

It's the part that pushes me away when we should be working on the problem together.

I know that he needs space, but I need the opposite of space.

I need him to take me in his arms and tell me that it's going to be okay.

Even if it's a lie.

There's a large boulder that sits at the curve in the road and I decide to take a break. I open the bottle of water, take a sip, and then throw a few handfuls in my face.

Though I don't have any answers to the questions rushing through my mind, the physical exercise and the gorgeous view of the valley below starts to put me at ease.

Then my phone rings.

I answer it without looking at the screen.

"I'm glad that I finally got you," the voice on the other end says.

I suddenly realize the terrible mistake that I have made. It's not Tyler at all.

"It's okay, you don't have to say anything. I just want you to know that you still owe us the debt."

"I don't owe you anything," I mumble.

"Your mother does. She hasn't paid a penny and you are the co-signer."

The way he says it makes it sound as if she borrowed the money from the bank. Unfortunately, she didn't.

"How is she?" I ask.

I haven't asked this question in a very long time, partly because I didn't want to know the answer.

"I don't know. She's missing. I thought maybe you would though."

"I haven't heard from her in a very long time."

"When will you have the money for us?"

"I don't know, but soon."

"You've been saying that for a long time," he says.

You would expect that his tone would be one of frustration, but it's almost as if he's used to making these calls.

"Listen, I don't need to actually threaten you for you to know how serious the situation is, do I?"

"No." I shake my head.

"Her debt is on your head. You don't pay us one hundred grand, normally that means that little parts of you are going to start disappearing."

A cold sweat runs down my back.

"I don't really know what to say to this," I mumble after a long pause.

"You don't have to say anything. I'm glad that you're not getting hysterical or overreacting by calling the police. Although, I get the sense that you can't really do that, can you?"

"What are you talking about?" I ask.

"I know that you're traveling with someone very special to you, a celebrity even."

More cold sweat runs down my back.

How could he know?

How could he know any of this?

"I have no idea what you're talking about."

"Be that as it may, my sources are very thorough and I just want you to know that we are very well aware of your relationship with Tyler McDermott and the fact that all of the law enforcement agencies in this country are looking for him. Here's the thing," he says with a little laugh. "The reward for his arrest just happens to be the exact amount of your mother's debt. Your debt. So, if you don't get us the money by Monday, then we're going to have to contact the FBI and tell them precisely where you are."

"You have no idea where we are," I say.

"Palm Desert, California. Staying at the Motel 6 down by 111."

I drop my phone and scramble to pick it up. When I finally get back on the line, he has already hung up.

27

ISABELLE
WHEN I GO BACK…

I don't want to go back to the motel. I don't want to see Tyler.

All I want to do is get into the car and drive as far away from here as possible, but I can't.

Tyler is in danger and despite everything that has happened, I owe him an explanation.

When I get back to the room, I have to knock a few times before he opens the door.

"You didn't have to leave like that," he says, clearly angry.

"I need to talk to you," I say quietly.

I put all my stuff on the other bed and sit down on the one that he has been lying on. Then I burst out crying.

The tears just flow out and I can't make them stop. I cry until my eyes get so puffy that it hurts to even rub them.

I cry until it feels like there are little razor blades pushing on my eyelids. I'm not just crying over all of the secrets that I have kept and all of the lies that I have told.

It's more than that or partly, it's less than that.

Have you ever experienced that feeling of exhaustion when you've just reached your breaking point?

I haven't slept well in days and I'm the type of person who needs deep, quiet sleep.

I miss my home and I miss my students.

I miss just going through my day without a worry in the world.

"I'm not cut out for this," I say quietly, wiping away tears as more and more come.

It hasn't even been that many days and I feel like I'm breaking.

"I'm really sorry," Tyler says, draping his arm over my shoulder. "We should've never done this. I love you, but you deserve so much more than this life on the road that's going nowhere."

"It's not just that," I say quietly. "I've been keeping some secrets from you and you deserve to know the truth."

He gives me a slight nod and waits for me to continue.

"I didn't just come with you out of the goodness of my heart. It's not that I don't love you, I do, but I also came here to get away. I thought that maybe they would stop bothering me if I wasn't there anymore."

"What are you talking about?" he asks calmly.

He's no longer absent or far away like he was earlier.

He's here with me.

Present.

Concerned.

Willing to help.

"Once you told me about Tessa, I thought that maybe I would have a way out of this mess."

I dry the last of my tears and move slightly away from him on the bed to face him.

"My mother owes a lot of money to some mafia guys. We haven't been in touch at all for the last couple of years, but she got addicted to painkillers and I knew that she'd gotten involved in selling drugs as well. Then she disappeared."

"Did you think that something had happened to her?"

"At first, I thought maybe, she does have this habit of ghosting me, not calling me back for days and weeks. So, I didn't think much of it. Then this guy started contacting me about paying her debt. I thought it was a joke, but then they kept pressuring me and insisting that I owed them $100,000. I had nothing close to that and I have no idea why I was expected to pay that in the first place. I ignored their calls and then they showed up at my door. I changed my number but the calls kept coming. I saw them as empty threats at first but after a while, it didn't seem to be that way anymore."

"Is that why you ran away?" Tyler asks.

I nod and say, "I should've known better. They found me here. They called me and said that I have until Monday to pay or they're going to really hurt me."

"Have they said that before?" he asks.

"It's different this time," I say.

"How?"

The Perfect Cover

This is the part that I have been dreading to tell him about. I lick my lips and look down at my ragged fingernails. I've been pretty good about not biting them for a while and then today, I just couldn't stop myself.

"They know about you," I say, looking straight into his eyes. I want this part to be untrue as much as possible, but he needs to know exactly what's going on.

"What are you talking about?" Tyler asks.

"He told me that he knows that we are traveling together. He mentioned you by name. He mentioned the reward money and how it's for the exact same amount that I owe him or rather what my mother owes him."

I expect Tyler to get angry, to jump up and yell at me. I don't know why I expect this to happen.

He has never been that way to me. Somehow, this is worse. I need him to be here with me.

To be present.

To connect with me.

With each passing moment, he seems to get further and further away.

"It doesn't have to mean anything," Tyler

says after a long pause. "He could be bluffing."

I don't believe that and I don't think he does either.

"He told me where we are right now," I say quietly. "While I was on my hike, he called and threatened me and told me to pay by Monday. He also mentioned this exact motel."

Tyler swallows hard and looks away from me.

"They know everything," I whisper. "I'm so sorry."

Tears start to roll down my cheeks and I wish more than anything that there was something I could do to make them stop.

"This has been a terrible mistake," Tyler says, staring somewhere out into the distance.

I don't know if he means meeting me or taking me with him or loving me at all. I'm too afraid to ask.

I wipe my tears away over and over again, but it's all to no avail. There are so many of them that I can barely see. So, when he gets closer to me and presses his lips onto mine, he takes me completely by surprise.

His lips feel soft and strong and he carefully guides my body back on the bed.

When he pulls away slightly, he raises his head up and kisses my cheeks. I blink a few times and see large droplets of tears, attached to my eyelashes. He brings his lips up to my eyelids and kisses those tears away.

When I look up at him, he whispers, "I love you."

"I love you, too," I say quickly, "but—"

"Shhh," he mumbles, putting his index finger onto my lips. "Let's not talk. Let's just be with each other."

My heart flutters as I feel my whole body connect with his. I wrap my arms around his strong powerful back and never want to let go.

After pulling away, we stand in front of each other and take our clothes off. My hands shake a little bit as I pull off my shirt and I feel his gaze focus on my body.

A familiar feeling of embarrassment takes over and I'm tempted to cover up my flabby stomach, but what I see in his eyes is anything but scorn or pity. Instead, he looks at me the way that people look at marble statues in museums. With adoration and awe.

"Why? Why do you look at me like that?" I ask.

"I just can't believe that you let me be with you," he says, shaking his head.

I blush.

"What are you talking about? Have you seen yourself?"

He gives me a happy smile. As I run my fingers up and down his six pack, he flexes his muscles and poses like David.

I laugh.

"No, seriously. You're so…hot."

"This," he points to himself, "is nothing. Just a body."

"A chiseled body that looks like it has been made from stone."

"No," he says, taking my hand and pulling me close to him. "You're the one that's beautiful. You're the one that's breathtaking and exquisite."

He pulls me over and on top of him. I like the view from up here. Tyler almost looks small in comparison. He grabs onto my butt and squeezes it tightly. Then he reaches over and cups my breasts.

The Perfect Cover

I've always hated being on top. Not only do I feel slightly uncoordinated being the one who instigates the movements and keeps the tempo, but I also don't like the way that my stomach and breasts move with each thrust.

Yet, when I look at those eyes, I know that he doesn't see any of that.

He wants me for me; the person underneath all this.

No, it's even better than that. He sees me for who I am and he loves that.

We kiss for a while and then he rolls on top of me and fishes out a condom from the pocket of his jeans. After he slips it on, he pulls me on top of him again.

"I want to see you," he says. "All of you."

I blush again and sit up. I prop myself up with my hands on his thighs and take him inside.

I start to move my body, slowly at first. I take him further and further inside and eventually my legs get tired.

I lean over him and kiss him and admit that I have been a failure.

He laughs, shaking his head.

"I can't believe that you're laughing at me," I whisper, kissing him again and moving my body up and down his cock as a way to accentuate my statement.

"Okay. Let me take over."

I let out a sigh of relief. I try to move over, but he stops me.

"What do you think you're doing?" he asks, shaking his head. "You're staying exactly where you are."

A thrill of excitement rushes through me.

I put my hands on his stomach, to brace myself as he starts to thrust himself faster and faster within me.

The speed with which he moves is nothing like what I had experienced before.

Within a few moments, I feel myself reaching the edge. I hold on tight as a warm soothing sensation rushes through my body. Instead of a soft wave, it's a tsunami.

A few moments later, he yells my name and relaxes his body. I fold over myself and collapse into his arms.

The Perfect Cover

AFTERWARD, lying in his arms, I feel like the world makes sense again even though it doesn't.

This was a temporary stop measure.

This was a Band-Aid on a bleeding wound. We still don't have any money to solve my problem or his and not many options with which to look into the future.

"Can I ask you a question?"

I nod.

"Why didn't you go to the police? When all of this was happening with your mom? When they first started making all of those threats? Before I showed up."

I sigh, letting out the air very slowly. This isn't something I wanted to talk about either, but it's time to come clean about everything that has happened, however painful.

"I couldn't," I say after a long pause.

He waits for me to explain without pushing me.

"I didn't feel safe. I didn't think they would do anything."

"What do you mean? Why?"

"I dated a cop at the Pittsburgh Police Department."

"Okay." He props himself up with the pillow.

The sheet falls over his torso, draping slightly over that place where his oblique muscles make a V. Glancing down, I kind of want him again.

"Isabelle?"

"Yeah," I say with a deep sigh.

I realize that I just want a distraction. Of course, I want him, but I also don't want to talk about this. This was one of the darkest periods of my life.

"What happened?" Tyler asks. "You dated a cop at the Pittsburgh PD. Did he do something?"

"Let's just say that he wasn't a really good guy," I say after a long pause. "He worked at the precinct that I would have to go to make a complaint about those phone calls. They would be the ones that would be investigating the situation."

"You didn't think that they could do it? Maybe they could make the mobsters back off?"

"No, they won't do that. The guy that I

dated got really possessive. I thought it was romantic at first that he was so jealous of every other guy that even looked at me or was interested in me. I was stupid and naïve. He told me what to do and at first, I didn't want to listen, but then I got scared. He was violent and he threw his fist through the walls on numerous occasions. I had a few friends, but I stopped hanging out with them due to having a fear of what might happen. He would just explode for no reason. I was embarrassed but I couldn't make him stop. The only thing I could do was pull away.

"Dating him was the worst time of my life. I had just broken up with my fiancé. It was just supposed to be a rebound guy. A few dates, that's it, but on the third day he came over and refused to leave. He threatened me, made jokes, and then hit me."

"I'm so sorry," Tyler says.

"I never thought I would be one of those women that would put up with that. I always thought that I was strong. I thought that I would never allow someone to treat me like that, but he had power and I was scared of that power. The first time that he punched me, I got a black eye and I went to make a report, but my precinct was his precinct. His friend took my statement and then kept pressuring me to drop the case. They kept saying how maybe I was confused. Maybe I was exaggerating. At first, they were thinly veiled threats but after a while, they were just threats. When he found out that I went to the police and told them what had been going on, he threw me against the wall. He told me that if I were to ever do anything like that again, he would kill me. I knew that no one would ever find my body. No one would ever know that I was even dead."

"I'm so sorry," Tyler whispers over and over again while rubbing my back.

I pull away from him. I can't have him touching me right now. Not if I want to get all of this out of me.

"Then things got worse," I say, hearing my voice crack.

"What happened?" he asks in that desperate quiet way that you do when you don't really want to know the truth, but you feel compelled to find out.

The Perfect Cover

"He invited me on a trip to New York and then kept me locked in that house for a week. He wouldn't let me leave. He did whatever he wanted and I couldn't make him stop. When I tried to go for a knife, when I tried to hurt him back, he caught me and he made things worse. I thought about going to the police after that, but if they didn't want to believe me about him hitting me, why would they want to believe that he did any of that?"

"So, what happened after?"

"I got really lucky and somebody else did." I pause for a moment, trying to gather my thoughts.

"He met someone else," I finally say. "He liked to go to this bar with his cop friends and he happened to hook up with this other girl and they hit it off. He left me for her and I have never been happier. It happened so fast that I just worry that something bad is happening to her, too. I was just out with her a few times, but she told me that she loved him and that was it. The fourth time that I called, he answered the phone and told me to stay away from them or he'd kill me. I decided that

I had given enough effort to try to protect her."

"I'm so sorry," Tyler says over and over again.

I wish that he would stop, but I know that there isn't much else to say to any of this.

I tell him that I kept evidence of what happened to me that week. I made videos and took photographs, just in case, but I never filed any charges because I didn't trust that police department to do anything for me ever.

"That's why I never told them about these threatening phone calls for the debt my mom owes. I just figured that they would somehow use it against me and I didn't want that to happen."

"Is that why you were afraid to leave the house when I met you?"

"Yeah," I say, looking up at the ceiling. "I got terrified of going anywhere where I didn't feel safe and I didn't feel safe anywhere. I stayed home as much as I could. It was the only place that I could. I was obsessed with controlling my environment because I had lost control so long ago. He made me not want to live. He made me afraid of my own shadow. Then *you* came along…"

He shakes his head and says, "If I had known that you had been traumatized like that, then I would've never snuck into your house. I would've never tied you up. That was so fucked up."

"You didn't know."

"It was a fucked up thing to do, regardless," Tyler says.

"You were trying to protect me," I say, exhaling slowly. "You didn't want me to know who you were. You had no idea that this had happened. Do you realize that, despite everything that has happened, despite everything that we have been through, I don't regret having you in my life for one minute?"

"You don't?"

"Do you?"

"No," he says, shaking his head vigorously from side to side. "I love you, Isabelle. You made me believe that the world is a good place. That's something that I had forgotten long ago."

"I love you, too, Tyler," I whisper and lean over and kiss him.

He reaches over and pulls me on top of him.

He kisses me over and over again and I kiss him back. Our bodies intertwine again, with only the sheets separating us from each other.

28

TYLER

WHEN WE GO BACK...

Later that evening, I decide to go back to see Tessa by myself. This time, I'm not going to take no for an answer.

After leaving Isabelle alone at the motel, I drive to Tessa's house and go over everything that Isabelle has told me in my head.

Now, I know why Isabelle had kept everything a secret. Now I know the shame that she has felt and how hard it was for her to get past it. When I park in front of Tessa's house, I promise myself that one way or another I'm going to pay off her debt.

When Tessa opens the door, she gives me a coy smile.

"You're back," she says, crossing her arms across her chest.

This time she's dressed in linen pants and a short sleeve shirt to match.

"Yes, I'm back. I have to talk to you."

"Come in," she says, spreading her arms out in a grand gesture.

"I know that I shouldn't have brought that up while Isabelle was here, but we've been traveling together and we've gotten really close."

"Tyler, let me interrupt you. I know that you think that I was making something up, but I wasn't. I was telling you the utmost truth."

"Tessa, we need the money. How else am I going to get a new identity? How else am I going to start a new life? I can't just go out there and get a job."

"I know and I feel for you. I will pay you every last cent, I promise. The problem is that all the money is tied up. I don't have it."

"You don't have credit cards?"

"Listen, I don't owe you an explanation beyond what I have already said."

"Yes, you do," I say, lowering my voice.

The Perfect Cover

"You owe me a lot more than this, but I'll accept this for now."

Her lips tighten as her jaw clenches up.

"I didn't have to keep that a secret. Who knows, maybe having an alibi would've prevented this whole mess from happening, but I kept my secret and I didn't tell anyone about you. You owe me. You owe me big."

There's a long pause that passes between us. After it's over it feels like something changes.

"Okay," she says, relaxing her shoulders. "I know that I owe you and I know that this is a really shitty situation. If I had known that you were coming, I wouldn't have touched it. How about this? I can give you a few thousand dollars and then you can do a job for me to get the rest."

"A job? What kind of job?"

"I have about 200 grand buried in the desert near Amboy. I have the directions, but it is in these barrels and it will require a bit of digging. As you can imagine, I can't really trust too many people with this information, so I haven't been able to retrieve it in quite some time."

I stand before her, flabbergasted. I have no idea how to respond.

"Do you want to do this or not?" Tessa asks.

No, actually I don't, I say to myself. What choice do I have?

"Why?" I ask.

"Why what?"

"Why do you have barrels of cash buried in the desert?"

She takes a step closer to me, narrowing her eyes. On the outside, Tessa looks like a middle school administrator: just friendly enough to put you at ease, but someone who is used to dealing with bullshit so she doesn't have much time for it.

"Do you really want an answer to that question?" Tessa asks after a long pause.

I don't need the details to know that it can't be anything good.

I shake my head.

"Good," she says. "Do you want the job or not?"

"What does it entail, exactly?"

"The three of us drive out to Amboy. I have the coordinates of the precise location.

You and Isabelle dig and get them out of the ground."

"Why is it in barrels?" I ask.

"It is in cash. They're all ones and fives."

"Ones and fives? Those barrels are going to be quite big."

"They are."

"All the money is there?"

"Yes," she says. "It's there for safekeeping, but I realize the predicament that I had put you into. I am sorry about that. You know me, I try to be as honest and fair as possible, despite how ugly our business is."

I hate the way that she says, 'our business'. I was never involved in drugs and guns and whatever else she does for a living.

"Yes," she says with a little plastic smile on her face. "I did say our business."

I glare at her.

It's almost as if she can read my mind.

"You were one of my biggest initial investors and I'll always appreciate that. I know that you don't like thinking of yourself as being involved in what I do, but please don't lie to yourself. This is what *you* do."

"With all due respect, Tessa, I ran a hedge

fund," I say after a long pause. "You borrowed some money, you invested in my business, I lent you some money and invested in yours. Never have I ever been involved in the drug trade."

"You know, you financiers are all the same," Tessa says, crossing her arms across her chest. "You think that just because you wear fancy suits and drive expensive cars and work in high-rises that your money is not out there circulating, doing your dirty deeds and making your percentages. Then, when you're in trouble, you come crawling to me."

"No," I say sternly. "I'm not coming to you for help. I came here to get paid. I came here for the money that you owe me. You said that you don't have it and now you're asking me to get my hands dirty to get it back."

I hate the way that this conversation is going. I would have never taken it here if she hadn't start pressing my buttons.

Despite all of our differences, I know that I have a long drive to Amboy ahead of me, with her in the passenger seat.

It's the only way that I can get out of this situation and start a new life with Isabelle.

29

ISABELLE

WHEN WE DRIVE TO AMBOY...

When Tyler comes back to the motel room and tells me that early the following morning we will be driving out to a town with a population of ten to retrieve some barrels full of cash, I am more than skeptical. But I'm also relieved.

If the barrels actually contain the money that we need, then that's great. Even though this money is in dollar bills or fives, that's better than nothing.

After a light dinner that I get from the diner next door, I sit by the air-conditioning vent and look out of the only window in the room. I can see the traffic outside on the busy highway rushing past the mountain. There's a stoplight not too far away that seems to get everyone going about sixty miles an hour to a squealing stop.

"I really miss staying in nice hotels," Tyler says, staring at his plastic fork when he tries to impale a crouton, and I laugh.

"Yeah, this must be something to get used to for you."

"You have no idea," he says.

"Tell me about it."

"Well, I grew up pretty well off. My father traveled a lot for work but he made a really good living."

The definition of a good living tends to vary a lot, so I ask for details.

"I think he made about $300k a year," he says, not blinking an eye. "He was defined by every last cent of that money. When I set out to make my fortune, I decided that I would never let money stand in the way. Yes, I wanted to make a lot, millions. The sky was the limit, but there were certain things that I would not do for money. I also wanted to never change my character."

"I don't think it has," I say after a long pause.

"No, unfortunately it has. I wasn't a good husband, not after a while. At first, we were really connected. We loved each other. I thought that I was going to spend an eternity with her. I was excited by that, but after a while, I got so busy with work. It consumed me. I wanted more and more. No number was big enough. Every day I had to make more money than I made the day before. Every quarter I had to top what I made the quarter before. My investors loved me. My wife? She started cheating on me."

"You're not responsible for her cheating," I say. "Just like the women who get cheated on, they're not at fault. It's always a cheater's fault."

"Be that as it may, I could have done better. I could have been there for her more. Instead, I was just there for my clients. People like Tessa."

"I know that she doesn't seem like the greatest person right about now, but it really says something that she is still paying you back the money."

"Do you think so?" he asks.

"Yeah," I say, putting the lid over the

plastic container that used to hold my dinner. "I don't know anything about the drug business, but I don't think it's populated with too many honest people, despite what television shows would want you to believe."

He puts his lips onto mine.

"You really are a good person, Isabelle. Don't ever doubt that."

I smile at him as he pulls me closer to him.

He kisses me again and again and I kiss him back. When he runs his fingers down my neck, I pull away.

"What's wrong?" he asks. "You're not in the mood?"

"No, it's not that. It's that I just got my period."

"That's okay." He smiles. "I don't mind."

"No, I can't. I'm all bloated and uncomfortable and my head hurts."

"Okay, let's just lie down in bed and I will hold you."

"That's it?" I ask.

He nods and grabs my hand, pulling me onto the bed and under the covers.

He wraps his body tightly around mine as

The Perfect Cover

I lie on my side. His knees fold under my knees and his arms drape over mine.

The moon comes out and peeks over the mountain outside. I close my eyes and fall into a deep peaceful sleep.

It takes about two hours to get to Amboy through some of the harshest desert I have ever seen.

Don't get me wrong, it's also beautiful, breathtaking, and wild.

We leave around nine and pick up Tessa along the way. We drive north through Yucca Valley and Joshua Tree and pass the US Marine Base in a town called 29 Palms, which only has two streetlights.

There's a large grocery store, Stater Brothers, and a few barber shops and tattoo parlors, all of which have large murals painted on the walls. Following the directions on the GPS that take us closer to the Marine base, we hear the bombs detonating out at the fake Iraqi town near the base.

The directions take us further into the

desert, where the creosote bushes flatten out and turn into sand. Another small settlement pops up, filled with nothing but a few cabins scattered on five-acre plots.

There are no stores or restaurants visible from the road and I remember reading that this place was founded by the Homestead Act from the 1950s, selling cheap land to anyone willing to build on it. After we pass Wonder Valley, we go over a long tall ridge and then dip down into an even drier and arid valley below.

I look out the window and lose myself. The lack of people and plethora of nature is comforting about this place. There are no tall trees or gorgeous mountain peaks, and the outside world appears to be almost nature in disguise. Maybe it's the fact that the nature is almost in disguise. It's uneven, rugged, and overwhelming and it brings a tear to my eye.

When I see a crater looming in the distance, I know that we are near Amboy. There's a small gas station and a few cottages that don't seem to be open for overnight visitors nearby.

Tyler takes a sharp left and drives toward

the crater. Millions of years ago a large asteroid hit this place, folding the earth upon itself. When I looked it up online, most of the sites were created by devotees of paranormal activities.

Right before we reach the crater, Tyler takes the road that veers right. This little car is not the best thing for driving out on the rough terrain, but it will have to do. I just hope that it can make it back out without overheating.

Once the drive is over, the three of us talk about anything and everything to fill the time. I'm surprised that Tessa has chosen us for this endeavor, but perhaps Tyler is right; there aren't many people that she can trust.

When we get there, a cold breeze sweeps over the imposing crater and I put on my flannel shirt. It's springtime and the sun feels unusually hot, but there is still a cold breeze that can startle you and chill you to your bones.

"There," Tessa says, pointing to a small rock laying on top of the ground.

It doesn't look like anything at first, but when you look closer, you can see that it doesn't quite belong here. It's black and made of smooth glass, very different from the sandstone and granite that surrounds it.

"There it is," Tessa says. "That's where I buried it."

Tyler opens the trunk and brings out two shovels that Tessa had in her garage. I wish that she would volunteer to help, but she doesn't. Instead she takes a few steps away from us in her linen suit and lights a cigarette.

Anger starts to rise up within me, but I refuse to succumb to it without first figuring out if the money is actually here.

I know that Tyler deserves a lot better than this, but beggars can't be choosers. Isn't that how the phrase goes?

I point the shovel down and step on it to drive it into the ground. The earth is as hard as a rock. It's not like the soft dark soil that I have back in Pennsylvania.

It feels like it's even harder than the ground would be under a layer of ice. Perhaps, that's an exaggeration, but I start to sweat profusely after only a few forceful scoops.

I glance at Tyler and see that he is doing a

lot better than I am. He is strong and powerful and continues to work without taking a break.

The only time he pauses is to take down some water and to take off his shirt. His six pack glistens in the desert sun and instead of chopping away at my section, I just want to grab him, press him against the car, and have him do bad things to me.

After almost an hour, Tyler's shovel finally hits something hard. He points at it and I kneel down and move some of the rocks and gravel away with my hands, revealing the top of the barrel.

"It's here!" I say excitedly. "It's here!"

Tessa walks over slowly and looks down into the hole.

"I told you."

I wait for her to get a little bit more enthused, but instead she turns her attention to her phone and finds some shade.

I don't care. It's finally going to happen, I say to myself. We're going to have the money and we can get as far away from here as possible.

About an hour more of back-breaking work, we finally pull the barrel out of the ground. Tessa walks over and opens the top. I look down to see what's inside; it's full of money.

Some of the bills are tied up with rubber bands, but most are just in stacked in piles. Ones and fives definitely do take up a lot of room.

When we put the lid back on and roll it over behind the car, Tessa points to another smooth black rock and tells us that the other barrel is here. Drenched in sweat and exhausted from the effort that I had already put in, I want to take a break.

Tyler refuses.

Instead, he gets straight back to work.

Just as we are about to pull the other barrel out of the ground, a car turns onto the dirt road that leads to our parking spot.

As it approaches, my heart starts to beat faster. It's driving too fast and kicks up too much dust to make out the make or model.

Tyler points to the car and asks, "Who is that?"

It takes a moment to realize what's happening, but then he furrows his brow and glares at Tessa.

The Perfect Cover

"Who did you call?" he hisses at her.

She shakes her head and she looks as surprised as we are.

Before anyone can do anything, the car comes to a sudden stop and three people get out.

"Hey there!" a familiar voice yells out and I realize that it belongs to Mac.

When he takes a few steps closer to me, I recognize the girl by his side.

It's Maggie.

The other man, tall and handsome, stands a little bit behind them and I don't know who he is.

"What are you doing here?" Tyler asks.

"Well, I came to collect my debt," Mac says.

"What are you talking about?" Tyler asks.

I glance over at Tessa who looks as confused as I do. I wonder if it's an act, but then the more that they talk, the more that I realize that this is something between Tyler and Mac.

"You owe me," Mac says. "For saving your life in prison and you owe me for what you and your girlfriend were about to do to us before we split."

"What are we going to do?" Tyler asks. "Who is he?"

"This is Nicholas Crawford. My partner. He helped me out of a jam, more than a few times, which isn't exactly what I can say about you."

"What are you talking about?" Tyler asks. "I was there for you in Hannibal. I picked you up when the whole world was looking for you."

"Yes, I'll give you that. You did, but I saved your life in prison and you still owe me for that. Besides, I need the money, you know I do."

"This money doesn't belong to you," Tyler says.

"Well, technically, it doesn't really belong to you either."

"Yes, it does. Tessa owes it to me and I'm taking it with me."

"No, you're not," Mac says, pulling out a gun.

Maggie takes a step away from him.

"Mac, put that gun down. C'mon, man," Nicholas says.

When I squint, I glance over at him and see the strong outline of his jaw and the straightness of his nose. His hair falls softly in his face.

Who is this mysterious stranger?

Mac doesn't listen. He shakes his head.

"Take that barrel and roll it this way," Mac says to Nicholas.

"Listen, I came out here as a favor, but I had no idea that you were going to be doing this. No, you've got to work this out in some other way."

When Mac refuses, he shakes his head and points the gun in Nicholas's face.

"Maggie, you better do as I say!" he yells over to her.

She does so without hesitation.

"Listen, Mac, let's talk about this," Tyler says, taking a step closer to him. "Whatever you think I owe you, we can work it out. There's enough money here for everyone."

"Take another step and I'm going to shoot," Mac threatens.

"Come on. We can talk about this. You're my oldest friend," Tyler says.

Bam!

The gun goes off.

The air gets filled with the smell of fire. I look at Tyler and watch him collapse onto the ground.

Thank you so much for reading THE PERFECT COVER!

I hope you are enjoying Tyler and Isabelle's story. Can't wait to find out what happens next? Their story continues in the next book.

Read THE PERFECT LIE now!

The Perfect Cover

WANT to know more about Nicholas Crawford? He has his own COMPLETE series that readers call "dangerous and impossible to put down."

Read TELL ME TO STOP now!

I owe him a debt. The kind money can't repay.

He wants something else: **me, for one year.**

But I don't even know who he is…

365 days and nights doing everything he wants…except that.

"I'm not going to sleep with you," I say categorically.

He laughs.

"I'm going to make you a promise," his eyes challenge mine. **"Before our time is up, you'll beg me for it."**

Read TELL ME TO STOP now!

WANT to dive into another EPIC romance right away?

Read ALL THE LIES now!

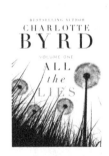

To save my job, I have to get an interview with a reclusive bestselling author who is impossible to find.

It's an insurmountable task until I get a lead. It's probably a joke but given what just happened in my personal life, it's an excuse to get away.

The last person I expect to see there is ***him*, the dashing and mysterious stranger** who was the only man who knew the truth *that* night.

He invites me inside under one condition: everything he says is off the record. He'll answers my questions but I can't write about him.

Then things get even more complicated. Something happens between us.

His touch ignites a spark. His eyes make me weak at the knees.

We can't do this.

But then he looks at me in that way that no one has ever looked at me and I can't say no…

Read ALL THE LIES now!

CONNECT WITH CHARLOTTE BYRD

Sign up for my **newsletter** to find out when I have new books!

You can also join my Facebook group, **Charlotte Byrd's Reader Club**, for exclusive giveaways and sneak peaks of future books.

I appreciate you sharing my books and telling your friends about them. Reviews help readers find my books! Please leave a review on your favorite site.

Sign up for my newsletter: https://www.subscribepage.com/byrdVIPList

Join my Facebook Group: https://www.facebook.com/groups/276340079439433/

Bonus Points: Follow me on BookBub and Goodreads!

ALSO BY CHARLOTTE BYRD

All books are available at ALL major retailers! If you can't find it, please email me at charlotte@charlotte-byrd.com

The Perfect Stranger Series
The Perfect Stranger
The Perfect Cover
The Perfect Lie
The Perfect Life
The Perfect Getaway
The Perfect Couple

All the Lies Series
All the Lies

All the Secrets
All the Doubts
All the Truths
All the Promises
All the Hopes

Tell me Series
Tell Me to Stop
Tell Me to Go
Tell Me to Stay
Tell Me to Run
Tell Me to Fight
Tell Me to Lie

Wedlocked Trilogy
Dangerous Engagement
Lethal Wedding
Fatal Wedding

Tangled Series
Tangled up in Ice
Tangled up in Pain
Tangled up in Lace
Tangled up in Hate
Tangled up in Love

The Perfect Cover

Black Series
Black Edge
Black Rules
Black Bounds
Black Contract
Black Limit

Not into you Duet
Not into you
Still not into you

Lavish Trilogy
Lavish Lies
Lavish Betrayal
Lavish Obsession

Standalone Novels
Dressing Mr. Dalton
Debt
Offer
Unknown

ABOUT CHARLOTTE BYRD

Charlotte Byrd is the bestselling author of romantic suspense novels. She has sold over 600,000 books and has been translated into five languages.

She lives near Palm Springs, California with her husband, son, and a toy Australian Shepherd. Charlotte is addicted to books and Netflix and she loves hot weather and crystal blue water.

Write her here:
charlotte@charlotte-byrd.com
Check out her books here:
www.charlotte-byrd.com
Connect with her here:
www.facebook.com/charlottebyrdbooks
www.instagram.com/charlottebyrdbooks
www.twitter.com/byrdauthor

Sign up for my newsletter: https://www.subscribepage.com/byrdVIPList

Join my Facebook Group: https://www.facebook.com/groups/276340079439433/

Bonus Points: Follow me on BookBub and Goodreads!

- facebook.com/charlottebyrdbooks
- twitter.com/byrdauthor
- instagram.com/charlottebyrdbooks
- bookbub.com/profile/charlotte-byrd

Made in the USA
Las Vegas, NV
09 June 2024